I0715761

# My Best Friend's Husband

# My Best Friend's Friend's Husband

## Joann Buie

Independently published by Desert Wind Press LLC
www.desertwindpress.com

ISBN 978-1-956271-32-4 (paperback)

ISBN 978-1-956271-33-1 (ebook)

# Contents

# Acknowledgments

Jim and Rose Dewey
Susan Dewey
Pam Mullenax Detrick
Vickie Allen
Barbara Meier
Sharon Brundrett
Nancy Gaede
Debbie Goodwin
Clarissa Buie
Cheryl Scott
Debbie Owen

# PROLOGUE



I could hear my name being called, or me being yelled at during most of my early childhood life. Pretty pathetic when I could hear them in my dreams so often, too. I wasn't really a bad child. Nor, did I do any physical harm to anyone either. But, I was hurting deep in my soul once my daddy had walked out on my mom and me when I was six years old, leaving me without knowing why he had done that, and what I had done wrong. At that time I didn't understand how he could do that to us, but later in life I learned he had been extremely hurt by my mother. I could not understand why he had to leave me behind though since I hadn't done anything bad all those years when he was with us.

I had decided then that I would act out to get attention, laughs from my classmates and other people, hoping my mother would send me to my dad's to live.

That was the plan in my head anyhow. It would have been a better place for me to grow up, but it never happened. Acting out was the only way I could deal with everything, and everyone in my life. But, that came to a halt one day when my mother and step-father had decided I needed to go away, and it wasn't to my dad's place.

I made the best of what I could growing up in that state home for "wayward children" by working hard in school to get the grades I needed to go to college to make a better life for myself after graduation. My mother never came to see me for a visit, or even inquired anything about me. That had hurt me more than what she would ever know, and probably ever cared. Maybe I reminded her of my dad, I don't know. All I knew was that I was on my own from then on. If I was dead to her, then she was dead to me.

My counselor had helped me fill out application after application to get a full ride to a college in other states. I received one that was in Ohio that I was more than happy to attend. Any place was better than staying with my bad memories I had while living in Virginia.

When I was about to finish college I met my first best friend in my life, Vivian. I needed money, and her and her husband needed someone to be a surrogate for their baby. Life made a complete change for me then, and it couldn't have come at a better time.

# SHENANIGANS

I had just heard the sad news about my best friend, Vivian. I was told she had passed away in her sleep last night. I couldn't believe it. How, why, or what had happened, no one was telling me. All I knew was that my best friend was forever gone. That news left me devastated. I had never had such a good friend my entire life, until I met Vivian. Vivian was the kindest person I had ever met. She helped me through so many obstacles in my young life, as well as confiding to me the things she was dealing with herself. She felt sure no one would believe her, nor understand the secrets she had shared with me. It seems as if I had done nothing, but cause problems for everyone around me, and maybe this was my punishment for those deeds in my past, I don't know.

## Where It All Began

All I do know is that I have been dealt a bad hand from the time my father walked out on my mom and myself when I was merely six years old. I didn't understand any of it at that age, and no one bothered to explain it to me. I remember my dad coming home from work and fighting with my mother before he packed all his clothes in garbage bags as he walked away from us. No good-bye to me, no tossing of my curly blonde hair, no nothing. He just left, but I did notice that it looked as if he had been crying, and he looked so sad when he walked past me. Something I will never forget about for the rest of my life.

Two days later my mother's new boyfriend, Buddy, moved in with us. It seemed as if I was in their way all the time no matter where I was, or what I was doing. I couldn't be quiet enough for them, couldn't eat quietly, couldn't breathe right, and received so many swats from the fly swatter, wooden spoon, or Buddy's brown leather belt. That was when I decided if I had to go through that kind of punishment, I might as well be bad enough to earn the swats that I was receiving on a daily basis.

I acted out in school more and more to get the attention of the teacher, so she would refer me to the office. Nothing matter to me anymore. I would laugh out loud over nothing, make barnyard animal noises when the teacher was trying to explain a new concept to us which resulted with the kids bursting out with laughter, to cheating on my Spelling tests by writing the answers on my pink eraser. It didn't matter what I did, I knew I was sure to be sent to the principal's office sooner or later. The poor teachers tried to redirect my poor choices, but it was just a waste their time.

At first, the principal tried talking with me as I sat there in front of her desk swallowed up in the big leather chair. Afterwards, she would ask me if I understood what she was saying. I'd smile, and shake my head to affirm that I had. I would then receive a small piece of candy before being sent back to the classroom. After a few months of her little chats with me, she actually thought maybe a few swats to my bottom would help more. I knew differently though. I just wanted another piece of candy, and get back to the classroom where I could find something new to do to get the teacher angry again.

I knew when that happened I had their undivided attention, and also knew it wouldn't be much longer until they would be calling my mother to come get me, and take me home. That was a gimmie to get out of classwork so I could play on my swing set in the backyard. What I didn't think was that when my mother got me home that I would receive swats from that leather belt by either her or Buddy. I hadn't thought that plan out very good, but I took those swats like a trooper without shedding a single tear. That made everyone even more mad at me, but I was determined they would never get a tear out of me when they dealt out the punishment. My last tears were shed the day my father had walked out.

It didn't take long before I was labeled as a troublemaker by everyone, and none of the teachers wanted me in their classrooms. My desk was always away from the other students, and I was in my own little world then. I continued with my antics daily in school and at home. I was going to show them that I knew what I was doing, and there wasn't a thing they could do to change me, or my attitude on anything.

It wasn't the easiest way to grow up not having anyone to play with at school, sitting alone at lunchtime every day, on the playground by myself, and being sent home so often with my mother. I missed out on fun activities during those times, but decided I didn't need anyone to be my friend, or have fun. It wasn't until I was in the sixth grade that everything really hit me.

I hadn't received a single valentine from anyone in my classroom. Not a single one!! I looked around watching everyone being happy with the valentines they had in their white decorated bags taped to their desks. I checked my little decorated bag one last time before I got into two girls valentine bags tearing all their valentines into little pieces when they were outside at recess.

Well, my teacher some how knew who had done that deed, and sent me to the office immediately when everyone came back inside, and those girls had started crying. I smiled at all of them as I walked out the classroom, and I marched to the principals office where I had to stay while everyone else was having fun with their classroom party in the afternoon. Not only did I not receive a single valentine, I missed out on all the wonderful treats the class had received. No one had saved any of the treats for me. Glad I tore the valentines up, and just laughed when the others talked about everything they received. But I was hurting, and for the first time in my life, I actually felt bad for destroying those valentines.

When I got home my mother and Buddy were furious with me, and it was shortly after that day that I was sent to a detention home for two weeks. Big mistake on their part is all I can say about that. I learned more rotten things to do for attention from the other kids there that I hadn't thought of doing myself, and they were really bad things. I couldn't wait to get home, and back to school to try them out for myself.

That summer was really tough for me, and before school started back up in September, my mother informed me she was pregnant, yet again. To top it off, they thought I was a dangerous kid to have around a newborn baby. I had never done anything dangerous to anyone, nor would I. I just did silly things that didn't hurt anyone physically.

Well, my mother and Buddy thought differently, and one day when I was playing on my swing set, two ladies came to my house. After they spoke with my mother and Buddy, I was called into the house, and had been told to get my clothes from my dresser and closet to put it all in a trash bag. I wasn't sure why, but did as I was told. Little did I know, but my mother had relinquished her parental rights of me to the state for them to take care of me from now on.

I just did as I was told not understanding why, and the what-for until I was in this large room in an old building those ladies had taken me to, and being told to put my clothes into this small locker by a bed, which wasn't even made. I was then told I needed to make the bed before going down the stairs to see someone else, which I did.

I sat there on a large wooden chair listening to this man telling me the rules of the place, and if I thought about running away from there, I'd better think twice about it. Also that the shenanigans I pulled at my old school, at home, or in the detention center would no longer be tolerated in any shape or form by him. I could tell he meant business with the tone of his loud voice he was using, and how his large hands slammed down on his desk several times. That was when it hit me what was going on. My mother didn't want me, so she got rid of me. I walked out of that office stunned at everything that was happening, and what that man had said about me. It was the first time I wanted to cry since my dad had left, but I refused to let that happen.

Fine, I will do everything on my own from now on, and I didn't need my mom or anyone in my life ever again. I could be as stubborn as I wanted, and I decided then and there to see what I could get away with, and how far I could push them.

The very next day I swapped out all the sugar in the sugar bowls by replacing them with salt on every table, and licked every spoon on the tables. I waited until lunch to see who would be my first victim. Much to my surprise, it was that fat man from yesterday who told me all the rules when I first arrived. Perfect person actually. I watched as he poured a large amount of the white substance from the sugar bowl into his mug of coffee. After a large gulp he spit it out, spraying it all over everyone around him while searching the room with his bulging eyes to see who had been watching him. I looked down immediately trying my best not to laugh, or have any eye contact with him.

It was only a few minutes later when he tapped me on my shoulder telling me to follow him. I smiled, and followed him to the office where he slammed the door shut. I cringed, and held my breath as he started to lecture me. It seemed like he knew that it was me who had been responsible for the sugar switched with salt. I tried to lie stating I didn't know what he was talking about. He brought up rule number three about telling a lie, and after several attempts to get me to confess, I wouldn't so he dropped that topic. He sat there twiddling his fat thumbs for a few seconds when he told me to wait outside as he called in an older lady to discuss me.

When she came out of that room she was visibly mad, and I hadn't done a single thing to her. She told me to follow her, which I did. I was placed in a small dark room with only a bed, and pail to do my business in. I entered the room, and she quickly closed the door behind her locking me inside. Wow! I knew this was my punishment, but didn't know for how long.

After my eyes had adjusted to the dim light, I saw a pillow and blanket on the bed that I quickly went over to. I wrapped the old scratchy blanket around me as I laid down on that damp smelly bed. My meals were brought to me by a kitchen staff member, and it was usually cold by the time I received it. It started to sink in with me that if I was to ever get out of here, I had better change my attitude, and study hard so I could leave this forsaken place. I didn't like it here, and I was going to get out of here one way or another. It was a long week in that dark smelly room, and I did think hard and long about my actions during that time.

Well, I did straighten out my behavior, and did my best to obey all the rules after that by thinking it would get me out of there, but it didn't happen. I ended up staying until I was out of high school. There was a wonderful lady that I had to talk to about my feelings that had befriended me some-what during my high school years. She had me apply to all these colleges for scholarships during my senior year thinking someone just might offer me a scholarship to attend their college. I had three letters from my professors as my required references, as well as one from her. I did as she asked of me thinking just maybe I would hear from someone.

And I did!! I received a full ride scholarship to a college in northern Ohio to obtain a business degree. I ran all the way to my counselors office to show her, and thank her so much for all her help. As soon as graduation from high school was over, I was on a bus to Ohio. I had the chance at a new beginning where no one would know me, and far enough away from my past in Virginia.

Since I arrived there during the summer months, I decided to take a few online classes that the college had offered, and I obtained a part time job for extra spending money for myself. There were plenty of places hiring for the summer with everyone gone from the dorm, and I printed out several resumes while I set up interviews from those that had responded.

I didn't have any trouble landing a job, and it looked promising for longer than the summer. I was hired as a receptionist at a dental office, and it was an easy job. I loved working there. I couldn't ask for anything better at this time. The pay was decent, and I planned to sock most of it away for when I finished college.

Between that I was living in the college dorm and working, I was kept pretty busy leaving me little time for socializing with other people, which didn't bother me that much. I was use to being alone most of my life, and learned to keep my nose clean some time ago. I wanted to get though college the best as I could, so I could have the life I always wanted.

I had a year to go until I was done with college, and after looking at my savings account, I realized I was short on my goal of what I thought I would need. After saving every pay check I earned, right down to the penny, I needed something else to help me reach that goal. I obtained a job on the weekends as a waitress at the nearby cafe to supplement the shortage. I was exhausted beyond words from all the hours I had worked. Luckily for me my grades didn't suffer from it, but I was really tired.

One day while working at the dentist office I saw an advertisement in the newspaper that caught my eye. It was for a couple that wanted to have children, but couldn't. They were seeking a woman to be a surrogate mother for them. They would negotiate the price, offer a small house to live in during the pregnancy, and pay all the medical expenses to the right person. A lengthy examination, and a contract would be involved. Nothing was said about the couple, and I figured it was just a scam. However, it did intrigue me some, and the more I thought about it, the more I was interested in doing it, if I ever got into a situation where I needed more money. I kept the paper, for what reason I wasn't sure.

When I went back to my dorm room that night, I had received some mail from the college finance department. There were some classes that they deemed unnecessary for me to take, and I would have to pay for them myself by the time I graduated, if I wanted to receive my degree.

I must have re-read that letter a dozen or more times before I called them to see what was going on, and why now of all times was I just hearing from them. I had followed their outline of classes I needed, so why should I have to foot the bill. I had followed their counselors advice to the tee on taking these classes, so it shouldn't fall back on me! A bill I couldn't afford even with all my savings. I had received a full scholarship on top of everything else. I set up an appointment to find out what was happening for the next afternoon.

Apparently, they had changed a few things last year never thinking it would affect me, but it had, and I demanded some answers. They repeated themselves over and over as if they had a script to go by, and repeated that if I wanted my degree in May, I had to come up with the additional amount of money. I didn't have any say in the manner, and I was at a loss of what to do. I needed that degree!

I left their office with an angry feeling that I had been taken advantage of, and made sure I slammed their door behind me hard enough to let them know just how mad I was. When I mentioned that I would fight it in court, they said to go ahead, but I would be throwing my money away because they would win. After a few days of sulking I gathered myself, and decided to do whatever I could do to get that money.

I tried getting a loan from different banks, but I was declined three times because I didn't have a job that they felt would qualify me for a loan. That was when I remembered that ad in the newspaper about becoming a surrogate mother. I thought it over for a few days, and decided to apply. It didn't mean I'd be chosen, and if I wasn't comfortable with anything I could always back out immediately.

I called the number listed on the newspaper ad. As I listened to the phone ring through, I had other thoughts running through my head. When the lady on the other end finally answered, I told her I was answering the ad in the newspaper for a surrogate mother. She was so kind telling me that I would need to fill out an application first. Once that was done, the couple will conduct an interview one on one with me, and go from there. She wouldn't give me any other information other than the man was an attorney, and his wife was a homemaker. I supplied the kind lady with my name and address so she could send me the application. Within three days I should have the application. She said I should be totally honest answering the questions, and supply anything else that would help me obtain an interview.

I could still back out at any time if I didn't feel it was on the up and up, or if I didn't feel comfortable with the questions being asked. At this point, I had nothing set in concrete, and they only had my name. Well, my address too, but they would have a hard time locating me on campus with my jobs and classes that kept me out of my room most of the time. I'm there only long enough to do a little studying, and to sleep.

When I went back to my dorm room a few days later, there was a letter waiting for me from an attorney's office. I knew what it was immediately, and quickly opened it. There was nothing about the couple like I had hoped for. Not even their name so I could check them out in advance, but the letter was from an attorney explaining everything they felt I needed to know.

I almost fell off my chair when they said the couple is willing to pay $20,000. They would pay $10,000 up front at the signing of a contract, and the rest after the delivery of their full term baby. That would definitely help me with my dilemma in more ways than one.

I started filling it out right away. By midnight I had finished it completely, and had it ready to mail back in the morning. Now, to wait for the next step of the process.

# The Long Process

I had another letter waiting for me by the end of the following week from the attorney's office. I wasn't sure if it really was on the up and up anymore. Nights of thinking that I had made a mistake filling out the questionnaire, a mistake that I could carry another persons baby, and the thought of just being pregnant itself just scared me to death. Then nightmares of being caught up in a money situation I didn't think I could get out of, nightmares of not being able to graduate from college, and not knowing what was in store for me next. Everything seemed to be tumbling down on me that past week, and I didn't know what I ought to do. I thought if I wasn't one hundred per cent sure about it, I would not do it.

I set the letter on the table as I made myself a cup of pipping hot tea hoping it would relax me a little, and maybe it would help me sleep through the night. I knew I just couldn't go on like this much longer without getting a decent night of sleep.

I placed my cup of tea on the end table as I opened the letter to see what it had to offer. Well, it looked promising, but there was another questionnaire they wanted answers to. I obliged by answering the first few questions, but at the end of the paper I stated that I didn't like giving out personal information like this. I needed more information about the couple other than the little snip-it that had been provided in their first letter if I was to continue to be a candidate on carrying their baby.

I left the papers on the table, but did not seal the envelope, and went back to bed. During the sleepless night I decided maybe I ought to send them a questionnaire myself to see if they were a fit for me. I needed to know something more about them. I had researched the attorney address, and it was legit, but was the proposition they were offering legit? I thought about the questions I wanted to ask them before falling asleep. I felt I'd put the ball back in their court, and send them my questionnaire the next morning.

I didn't like this cat and mouse game that it seemed to have been going on. I had two months left of college, and I needed answers, or a miracle to happen in my favor as soon as possible. In the meantime, I would have to work my butt off to get as close as I could to having the money needed for my classes. Talk about being up a creek without a paddle, that was how I was feeling.

After the week had passed of not hearing anything

more from the attorney's office, I figured that me wanting some information about the couple went over like a bowl of sour lemons. I didn't feel bad sending it because I was putting a lot of information out there about myself that could be used in other ways. I didn't have anyone to watch my back. I was alone in this situation.

However, when I went home that night after work, there was a letter waiting for me, and I couldn't wait to open it. I found my questionnaire immediately. It hadn't been answered at all. Not one single question had been answered. What a waste of my time, and effort to learn what I could about this couple. I almost just threw everything in the trash can when I saw that the letter was longer than usual from the attorney, and decided to read it anyhow.

It was a good thing I hadn't tossed it after all. The attorney wanted to meet with me in his office where we could have a one on one chat. There was a good chance I might meet with the couple as well, if that was acceptable with me. The couple understood my apprehension on answering anymore questions without something in return. All I had to do was call his office to set up a time, and also keep in mind it might be a longer than a normal attorney-client meeting, so I would need to take that into consideration on my class or work schedule.

Well, that wasn't what I had expected, but my time and effort had been considered by them now. I knew I could do it on Friday, in two days, where I wouldn't miss any classes or work because my classes were done on line, and

I could get that out quickly the night before. I also didn't have to work until later that night. Now all I had to do was see if they could comply with that day and time as well.

The next morning when I called the attorney, Andrew Williamson, had agreed to the day and time without even asking the couple. He said he looked forward to meeting with me, and even suggested that if I had questions I wanted to ask, to have them ready because he would answer them then. Oh, I had questions alright. I had jotted them down on paper the next two days when I thought of them, including the ones on the questionnaire I had previously sent them. After all, I had a lot at stake here as well.

The next two days felt like they flew by faster than normal. It wasn't until Friday early morning that I started to feel sick to my stomach from being nervous. I was a basket case by the time I left my dorm room to head downtown to the attorney's office for the meeting. I made sure I wore an appropriate outfit to give a good first impression without overdoing it, but I still felt something was missing. As I got off the bus close to the office, I realized I didn't have the confidence I thought I should have at this point. I saw a bench in the park close by, and quickly sat down for a few minutes to gather my wits and strength to continue on.

Finally, I decided it was now or never so I got up, and before long I was sitting in a small conference room waiting to be seen. I looked around taking in the room, and it's contents. There was a framed mirror on the inside wall. I knew it had to be for someone on the other side to view as to what was being said in the room I was waiting in.

After what seemed forever, the door finally opened. It was just the attorney, no one else. He introduced himself to me as Andrew, but prefers to be called Drew, who would be answering my questions, and asking more questions. He was very polite, and I could feel a kindness from him immediately.

It was a rough start with the questions at first, and after answering about ten of them I was able to ask questions of my own. I made several notes on my paper with some questions he wasn't able to answer right away. I could tell some of them made him feel uncomfortable, so after several that he didn't answer, I just blurted out why all the secrecy of this couple when they wanted to know everything about me. It wasn't what I had expected to happen at that meeting, and thought maybe I'd better leave so I wouldn't waste anymore of his time, or mine.

As I stood up to leave, he stood immediately with a shocked look on his face. At that time the door quickly opened. A lady entered with tears in her eyes as she pleaded with me to please stay. I was so dumbfounded with all the commotion happening right then. I wasn't sure if I should sit back down, or run as fast as I could out of there. What the heck was going on? Drew quickly rushed over to this lady putting his arms around her shoulders as she sobbed. Oh, I needed to run and run fast, but my legs refused to move.

Drew gave her a tissue right away once as she sat down

in the chair next to him. She reached across the table placing her hand over mine as in a friendly manner introducing herself as Vivian, Drew's wife, and they were the couple seeking the help to find a surrogate. I slowly pulled my hand away from her as she continued to explain everything. They hadn't thought about what their secrecy had presented to the potential surrogates, until she had watched from the other side of the wall through that mirror. That was when she knew they needed to come clean with everything, and why their importance of the meeting with me.

I had been the one that they had considered as the best candidate to interview, but they needed more answers from me. So when I called, they were excited that I had answered, even though they hadn't answered my questionnaire themselves.

Once I agreed to stay at the meeting, understanding that they wanted their answers and reasons to be kept strictly confidential, they had opened up on everything I needed to know. Vivian hadn't stopped crying until she explained that they wanted a family very much. They were able to conceive a baby, but for some strange reason Vivian's body would reject the pregnancy by the beginning of the fourth month, resulting in miscarriages. After several attempts to have a baby on their own, it was clear to see that she would never be able to carry a full term baby. The doctor suggested adoption which they had considered. The doctor also suggested trying a surrogate mother, which he thought might be a different approach, but possible. It would be Drew and Vivian's baby completely, just hosted in another body.

Drew and Vivian talked about it for several weeks before they had agreed to it, and placed the ad in the newspaper. They received several applicants, but there were a few women doing it for the wrong reasons, or they had a sketchy background that was worrisome for Vivian and Drew. Until they received mine, and liked what they had read.

That was when I confessed about being relinquished to the state by my mother when I was twelve years old, which I hadn't put in the letter. Maybe that would make my past as sketchy as some of the other applicants, or me undesirable for their choice.

It wasn't a factor in their choice at all, because with Drew being an attorney, he did a complete background check on me, and they knew about it already. I explained I wouldn't have done all those shenanigans as a child, but I had the class laughing, and it felt good for me to laugh as well. It had been a very sad time in my life.

After we sat there talking, allowing ourselves be human, we had a nice meeting. I left there feeling much better about everything, and we set a dinner date for next week Wednesday at their house. I left with their address, and home phone number in case something came up, but I was looking forward to going.

I thought over all the things they were asking of me, which was a lot. Especially about keeping everything extremely confidential. I didn't have a problem with that. What I thought was confusing was the fact that the only other person who would know who I was, and why I was doing this would be their doctor. That part I didn't understand clearly, and thought I needed more clarification as to why.

I went to my classes and work just like I had always done. The only thing now was my upcoming appointments with Drew and Vivian. I had no reason to tell anyone what I was considering. I wasn't sure about it one hundred per cent myself yet.

I went to dinner at their house that Wednesday. What a beautiful house it was at that. Nice, big, and decorated with great taste. When I walked to the door, they both greeted me by giving me a hug. I felt welcomed immediately, and it was as if I had visited with them for years. The dinner was amazingly delicious, and very filling. Vivian took me on a tour of the house pointing out several features that was becoming of the old house. It definitely was an old house, but I could tell it has been kept up very well.

I asked if I could see the little house in the back that they had spoke about, if everything went right, that I would be living in rent free. The small house was older than the big house they were living in by two years. As the larger house was being built, the owners lived in the smaller house, and it was kept for guests to stay in once the larger home was completed.

The smaller house was perfect in every way as far as I was concerned. It was small, consisting of a separate kitchen, living area, bedroom, bathroom, and a full basement. The bedroom had a deck outside the arcadia doors with two high back rocking chairs facing the back field to enjoy the sunset, and privacy. I didn't need much, and it was completely newly furnished so that was one less thing for me to worry about. There was also a small single car attached garage on the kitchen end of the house with the stairs that led to the basement.

We discussed a few other things, but Drew wanted to just relax, and enjoy each others company. We talked about a variety of things, and gave our opinions on several newsworthy topics. After dessert I decided I should leave, so I can make it back before curfew at the dorm.

We set a date, for another meeting to talk more, so we could get the ball rolling, and sign the contract, if I decided to accept their offer. Vivian handed me a present they thought I'd like. It was a cell phone, so we could call or text each other whenever we wanted. A full year free of charges. I was surprised with it, and at the same time I was happy to have one of my own cell phones. They hugged me goodbye, and I returned to my dorm room in time.

It was the first time I felt good about everything happening in my life. I felt a heavy weight had been lifted off my shoulders as far as paying my student loan on time for graduation, and it definitely helped me that night with sleeping. A good solid sleep, which I had needed for several nights. When I woke up I felt refreshed, and actually happy for the first time in a long time.

I received another notice about my so-called loan from the college. I replied I would have some money for them within the next few weeks. My happy bubble burst right then with their billing department being so demanding, but I had a feeling everything was going to be alright for some reason. It was a good feeling, and I decided I didn't need that notice to ruin my day. I chose to keep it a good day.

Vivian had texted me a few times to chat. She had a couple more questions she wanted to ask me, so she offered to take me out for lunch. I had the time that day, so we met at a diner that we didn't think would be too busy, but close to the college. I wasn't nervous to meet with her this time. Maybe because we had started a friendship since that night at their house last week.

Her questions were very basic. Mostly thought it would be better to talk woman to woman, without a man sitting there making things awkward at times. She mostly wanted to know if I have had many boyfriends in the past, and if I had ever taken any illicit drugs. I smiled at her telling her that I have never had a boyfriend, and I had never done drugs either. She asked a few other personal questions on dating, and if having a baby would bother anyone in my family. She was glad with the answers I gave her. I don't have time to date between classes and working. As far as having a family, I have a mother, but she and her husband were the ones who had the state take me away. She got rid of my father when I was six years old. I hadn't fit into their lives since I was twelve, and I didn't plan to see them ever again.

So, with the answers from me, I felt I could ask her one as well. I asked why they weren't telling anyone other than their doctor about me. Wow! I didn't expect what she had told me, but apparently they had wanted to make this pregnancy as realistic as possible. She was going to have a fake belly throughout the pregnancy. She had failed to carry any baby past her first trimester, and felt like a failure as a mother, and as a wife. A few family members had made their snide comments that maybe they weren't meant to be a family, and to get over it. "Get over it" stung in my ears. Such a cruel thing to say to anyone, no matter what the circumstances were. Drew and Vivian had wanted a family very much, and they just didn't feel the need for anyone else to know any different.

Since I will be living in the little house out back, after I deliver the baby, they would like me to wear the fake belly for about four to six weeks longer so no one would put two and two together about them suddenly having a baby, and I didn't.

I thought it over wondering if I was getting myself into another mess that I couldn't get out of. Or were the messes I had in my life going to continue to follow me forever.

I would be able to come and go as I liked while living in their little house, and have friends over when I wanted. They didn't have to worry about me having friends over because I really didn't have any. I had a few that I considered acquaintances, but they were not what I considered friends. Vivian thought that was so sad to hear, and immediately said that I did have a friend now, and it was her.

Vivian also noted that they would like to attend all my

doctor check-ups with me, and be in the delivery room when their baby was born. I didn't have any problems with that since it was their baby, and they had every right to be sure everything was going fine. What parents wouldn't want to know everything?

At the next meeting, which was in Drew's office, they went over the contract with me page by page. I knew I was going to do this for them. If I could make a couple become parents, I felt I would be doing something right in my lifetime. The contract was pretty simple to understand, and before I signed on the dotted line of accepting it, I asked if it was going to be a problem with them if I continued working at the dentist office until our due date. They didn't have a problem with that, unless it became too much for me. They would like me to take a leave of absence during the last month of the pregnancy to relax, and prepare myself for the childbirth.

Drew said that they could amend anything on the contract as it goes, providing that we all agree on it. With that being said, I wasn't hesitant when I signed the contract. Drew handed me a check for ten thousand dollars, and we agreed on our next meeting at the doctor's office.

Vivian explained that their doctor will be performing the necessary procedure to impregnate me. I assured them I would be there, before I left the attorney's office. Vivian hugged me thanking me over and over. Drew hugged me saying they would be sure I would be taken care of completely. Both Vivian and Drew were very happy. Vivian even shed a few tears of happiness.

I immediately deposited their check in my bank account, and made it back to the dorm so I could pay my outstanding bill. In two weeks I will be a graduate, and be out of the dorm completely. I couldn't wait to move into the little house.

# $\mathcal{N}$EW $\mathcal{B}$EGINNING

I couldn't wait for graduation to receive my degree that I had worked hard for. I gave my notice at the diner on the day I paid my college bill off. The owners were sad to see me leave, but said if I ever wanted to come back I could.

The week before I was to graduate, I met Drew and Vivian at the doctor's office. The doctor was very kind, and understanding of the situation I was about to do for the Williamsons. I felt very much at ease with him as he explained the entire process with me. We set the date to perform the procedure for the following week, according to my cycle. I asked Vivian and Drew to be there with me if they would like, and they were excited to be included. They could be in the room, but the doctor explained they wouldn't be able to be at the table while the procedure was being conducted. They didn't have a problem with that, and neither did I.

In a few days I will have the procedure done, and cross our fingers it will work on the first try. I actually had a smile on my face when the three of us left the doctor's office that day. We immediately went to the hospital to get the pre-admission paperwork completed and out of the way, and agreed on the time to meet there in a few days for the procedure.

I was ready for this journey to start, and I was happy to make a good thing happen for a wonderful couple. I would carry their baby, and know in my heart that I will always be a part of its life. That was one of the things stipulated in the contract, I would always be welcomed to all the functions for their child, and holidays with everyone.

I met them at the hospital early that morning, and we walked into the hospital together. I changed into the gown the nurse had provided, and was sitting on the edge of my bed when Vivian and Drew were able to come in. Vivian looked at her watch stating it was almost time for the nurses to come get me, but she wanted to know if she could do a little prayer before I was taken into the surgery room. I had no problem with that, and was rather glad she had said a prayer. I was beginning to get nervous, and scared at the same time. I had never been sedated before in my entire life, and had that running around in my brain as well of the possible things that could go wrong, and I wouldn't even know.

Once I was ready in the surgical room, Vivian and Drew were escorted in. They both came over to hug me before taking their place by the wall. When the doctor came in he assured me things will be fine, and I'll be out of there in no time. I had been given something to relax me right away which worked fast because I had a cloudy head, didn't feel any pain, and it was over quickly like he had said it would be. Once I was covered up with a nice warm blanket, Vivian and Drew were by my side thanking me for what I had just done for them.

I had to stay a few hours in the recovery room, but they could join me there. It was just for precautions, and for the sedative to wear off. I felt fine in about two hours. Was I expecting to feel something though? I don't know, but I thought it was easy peasy so far on my part. Vivian drove me to my dorm with Drew following us in my car. They helped me inside my dorm room where I was to rest for the next few hours. They assured me that they'd see me at my graduation before they left to go home. I rested for the remainder of the day, and the next until it was time to go to my finals. I felt great, and didn't have any discomfort like the doctor said I might have.

Graduation day was over before I knew it. I was so happy for it to be done. I had my dorm room almost packed, and ready to move into my little house. Drew and Vivian came to my graduation program. It was so nice having someone there for me.

After the commencement program was over, they took me out to a very nice restaurant to celebrate. I couldn't have been any more happier than what I was that day. They were so kind, and genuinely happy for me to graduate, and also for what I had done for them. Things couldn't have been better. Maybe that curse, and the black cloud lingering over me was now gone, and I would have a wonderful life ahead of me. I could only hope that the choices I had made will help me achieve my goals in life.

There were several parties going on in the dorm when I returned that night after dinner. Everyone was happy to be through with their education, and had celebrated most of the night. I was content to stay in my room to finish packing for my move in the morning. Once I had everything done I tried to sleep. Lord knows I needed to get some sleep, but with the commotion going on outside my door made it difficult. I had several things running through my head at the same time. My move to the little house outside the city, my job at the dentist office while being pregnant, and the pregnancy itself. I could only think of the best, and prayed things will turn out the way they should.

My move the next morning was a struggle. There were empty solo cups, and paper plates all over the hallway floors from the celebrations through the night. Even a few bodies were scattered around on the floors from those not being able to drive anywhere while being as intoxicated as they had been. I just had to be careful not to stumble over anything, or anyone while taking the boxes down to my car. I was glad I was able to fit everything into my car in one trip. I handed my dorm keys in at the dorm office, and received my clearance that I could officially leave.

At first I thought I would be sad. Actually, it was a

bittersweet moment for me. I had lived there for four years, and I considered it my home during that entire time. Now, I had to start over in another place, and make all the adjustments once again. But, I was ready as I pulled away from my assigned parking space. It didn't take me long to get off campus, and head out of the city.

I arrived at Drew and Vivian's house at lunchtime, which I should have thought through beforehand. I didn't want to interrupt their lunch, and I should have stopped at the store to get a few things myself for the next few days, until I could do my heavy shopping. I thought about this as I rang their doorbell, but I was too late in thinking about that now. Vivian answered the door, and was all smiles welcoming me in.

They had a housekeeper that worked during the week days that I was introduced to. You know that saying, that the first impressions are usually the more accurate ones? Well, this is how I felt about Velma when I was introduced to her. I felt a stand-offish-stay-away-from-me feeling about her immediately. One of not trusting, and definitely not one I wanted to make friends with. I would be cordial, and nice, but keep my guard up around her. A terrible thing to think about someone like that on the first time being introduced to her at the house, but that was how I felt. When Vivian introduced me to Velma, I had I extended my hand to her, but Velma never took it. Vivian rolled her eyes, but continued on telling Velma I was going to rent the house out back for a year or so.

Velma looked towards me announcing that she doesn't

get paid to keep my place tidy, do my laundry, or cook any meals for me. I smiled replying I never had expected her to.

I was trying to be nice, but I felt like telling her off at that moment, so I said I would be able to handle those chores myself without a problem. I also thought this was the perfect time that I should tell Velma that I also like my privacy, and expected to receive it as well. I could see Vivian out of the corner of my eye smile before she asked me to join her for lunch on the back patio. Velma had already made a tray full of sandwiches, and had two glasses of iced tea already on the patio table. Vivian explained that Drew had been called to the office, so there was plenty of food. Velma refused to join us for lunch which didn't hurt my feelings what-so-ever!

Lunch was very pleasant, and Vivian said she had to apologize for Velma's coldness towards me. I could sense that there was a little friction between the two of them right away, but I didn't feel it was anything I needed to know about, or any of my business. I replied that it had been fine, and not to worry about it. Vivian did explain that Velma had wanted to live in the little house when she first started working for them last year, but Drew denied her request. So I knew then I already had a strike against me by moving in there, but it wasn't my fault. In time I wondered if Velma would get over that.

After lunch I drove my car around to the back, parking it in front of the attached garage of my little house. Vivian had walked down from her house handing me the keys, and garage door opener to the place. I opened the garage door to take the boxes inside through the kitchen side of the house with Vivian helping me.

Vivian asked me to come outside away from the house saying we had better come up with a rental amount. At first I didn't understand why, and questioned her that I thought the house was part of the deal. Vivian shook her head yes, and continued with a chuckle. She said her mouth was getting ahead of her thoughts once again. Yes, it is part of the agreement, but just in case Velma would ask how much I'm paying, that we would be on the same page for the amount. Ohhh!! I understood now. I thought Vivian should be the source to come up with an amount, and she did. Four hundred fifty dollars a month with utilities included. I shook my head that it sounded good to me, but why would Velma ask a personal question like that, I wondered. Vivian said to be careful around Velma because she was sneaky like a fox. That was a strange thing to say, but also good to be warned!

Later that afternoon when I was making my bed I thought it was rather strange that Vivian asked me to come away from the house to talk to me about the rental amount. What the heck was going on here? Have I walked into a spider web of problems concerning Velma? I let out a heavy sigh, and knew I needed to watch my words around **everyone** while I continued to get my house set up the way I wanted!

Drew arrived home from his office before I was done unpacking, and came down to see if I needed any help. I had most of it already done, and there was nothing that I needed help with, so he invited me to come up to the house around six to have dinner with them before he left. He was grilling some steaks, and Vivian had made a potato salad earlier that afternoon to go with the dinner. I thanked him saying I'd be there offering to bring something. He smiled saying just my appetite would be all I needed to bring. Whew! That was a good thing because I didn't have anything I could make in the cupboards yet!

By the time I needed to walk up to the house for dinner, I had almost all the boxes unpacked, everything in the right rooms, the boxes broken down, and in the garage to be hauled to the garbage bin later.

I helped Vivian carry the dishes and potato salad out to the patio table. Drew was already busy with the steaks on the grill, and requested on how I liked mine prepared. I had never been asked that before, so I told him however they liked theirs was fine with me. He cocked his head smiling telling me they eat them rather rare, until he saw the look on my face. He laughed out loud stating he thought that would throw me a little. I laughed replying that it had. Then I asked how do they really like their steaks grilled. He said they preferred medium to medium well. That sounded so much better than rare, and I said that would be fine with me, too. Heck, I didn't know what medium to medium well was, but I knew it had to be better than rare!

And they were absolutely delicious as I ate every bit of my steak. Everything was perfect as far as I was concerned. Drew said they grill out every Saturday night giving me an open invitation to join them as well. I thought for a second wondering if he realized that it was Friday, not Saturday. He looked at me as if he read my mind adding that they were eating tonight as a celebration of my moving in. They knew I wouldn't have had the time to shop for groceries, yet.

Apparently Drew loved to cook, and especially grilling outside whenever he could. When I thanked them for the wonderful meal they had prepared, Drew reached across the table placing his hand over mine saying they meant it. I was part of their family now. Family. Wow, that really made me feel good that they had included me in as their family. It was something I will have to get use to, that was for sure!

Vivian told Drew how Velma had acted towards me when I arrived in the afternoon. He apologized for her rude behavior, and her lack of friendliness. I just nodded saying it wasn't a big deal. But, inside my brain I knew it was a warning to be careful around Velma. I wasn't going to let Velma ruin my night with Drew and Vivian either. I enjoyed their friendship and kindness. Vivian had made a delicious chocolate desert that was heavenly, and made the whole evening absolutely fantastic.

We moved over to the gas fire pit where Drew turned it on. We sat there talking about everything until about midnight on every topic possible. I noticed that whenever I talked about anything, they actually listened. I hadn't had that before, and I knew it was genuine. Not that I had much social time to visit with anyone to begin with, but it was really nice. It was as if my thoughts and opinions were validated.

I yawned saying I better get myself back to the house, and get to sleep. I saw Vivian was getting tired as well, so it was the end of our great time together. Both Vivian and Drew walked me to my home giving me a hug goodnight at the door. When I went inside, I knew I couldn't stay up much longer, and went to bed where I crashed into a deep sleep.

The next morning I heard plenty of birds outside in the wooded area behind my little house. A few birds were resting on the window ledge as if they were welcoming me there, and reminding me that I needed to get up. Their sweet chirping was really nice, and I thought that when I went to town to get my groceries later that I would also buy a bird feeder, and seed for my little feathered friends. I jotted that on my list so I wouldn't forget. My list was long, but my cupboards and refrigerator were bare. The doctor advised me that I should eat as many fruit and vegetables as I could, and to go lightly on starchy, salty, and sweet foods. I planned to follow his advise.

I asked Drew if it would be okay to walk the field further down from my house. I had noticed a path was worn in the dirt from a vehicle of some sort yesterday while unpacking. It was his property, and he had no problem with me walking it. Vivian said she might join me a few times, if I was okay with that. On the days she didn't walk with me I could put my earbuds in my ears listening to my music while I walked. It would make the walk very enjoyable, and go by faster.

After what seemed like I bought the store out, I placed

everything in the kitchen cupboards. They were full now, and should last me a few weeks. I bought two bird feeders with hooks on a string for them to hang from the rafters outside my windows so I could enjoy watching them. As soon as I filled the feeders, a lot of birds flew to them, and started chowing away. I had a variety of birds in every color, and I was glad I had bought the feeders. My contribution of helping the wild life here I suppose.

I made a chicken salad sandwich for lunch, and ate it while sitting in one of the high back rocking chairs on my deck off my bedroom. Once I finished my glass of iced tea, and finished unpacking the remaining two boxes, I decided to check out the path around the field. It was so nice and relaxing, but it was way too hot to walk it during the day. After supper would be a much better time when it has cooled off a bit, and just before sunset.

I had to go back to work in a week, and thought I would change my address information then. If this procedure works, and I am pregnant, after a few months I will inform my boss of that information, but not all of the information will be given. I don't see any reason to tell him I am a surrogate mother for a couple because I know that information would go through the office like a wild fire. Nothing is kept sacred in that place. That I learned the hard way when I said something that apparently offended one of the techs there, and overheard about it loud and clear later. So, I just stick to my job, keep my mouth shut, and don't ask anything of anyone.

I would know in five weeks if the procedure had

worked, and if I was pregnant. The doctor will take a blood test to have that confirmed. Vivian and Drew have made the appointments in advance for us to attend together. I wrote them all down on my personal purse size calendar so I wouldn't forget, which wasn't likely to happen anyhow. Vivian and Drew both had commented that I shouldn't leave anything out in the open that someone might see, and use to gossip about. That someone they were referring to was Velma, but why should she be in my house anyhow? She had made it clear she wouldn't be doing any cleaning or cooking in my house, and I had also made it crystal clear that I liked my privacy when we had first met. I couldn't understand why they just didn't fire her if they had a trust issue, and with her having a bad attitude toward them. I would think the housekeeper should be someone you could trust, but for some reason or another they had their reasons.

Vivian came over just about every other night to see how I was doing, or if I needed anything. One night she asked to walk with me. I could tell something was on her mind immediately. Once we got away from the house she asked if she could say something bizarre. Why not, but my mind started thinking creepy thoughts right away. What could she ask that would qualify as "bizarre", I wondered. She went into her thoughts, and asked if I ever felt like someone was listening in on my life, like they had the gift of foreseeing things in the future or past. I wasn't following her thought process right away, and asked her to explain what she meant. She told me that it had happened more than just a few times to her. It's almost happening every few days during the week that Velma would ask how Vivian liked a movie she had watched without Vivian telling her she even watched a movie.

That was bizarre for sure. I could see if Velma had asked if Vivian had watched a certain movie to get her opinion on it, but some how knowing Vivian had watched it the night before was rather creepy. Vivian would chuckle, and asked Velma if she had a sixth sense or something. Vivian wanted to know if I believed in a sixth sense, which I had never thought about in my entire life. When I told her I wasn't sure about any of that, Vivian quickly asked if I thought she was crazy to think something wasn't right.

She was worried that maybe with everything bad that has happened in her life with all her miscarriages and such, that maybe she was a little bit on the crazy side before she burst into tears. I stopped walking immediately and consoled her by telling her she was not even close to being a crazy person. I didn't have an explanation for Velma knowing what movie Vivian had watched, but I knew Vivian wasn't crazy. Poor thing was really upset saying she didn't have anyone to talk to about this that would be honest with her, or they'd just change the subject to something else.

We talked all the way around the property line, and I think Vivian was feeling much better by the time we got back to my house. We sat on the deck with cold iced tea talking more, but not about Velma. I couldn't help but feel bad for Vivian. I didn't have good feelings about Velma myself from the very first day I arrived, but I wasn't in the position to get involved too much where Velma was concerned. I could definitely be a good listener for Vivian though.

Vivian did explain why they hadn't fired Velma yet. Drew had come up with a program to help people down on their luck by working with them to get themselves back into the work force. He was the first to establish the program last year by hiring Velma for the next three years with other colleagues in his office following his example. So, they were basically "stuck" with Velma working for them. Unless she does something really dangerous, or steals from them, she was there. Drew had felt it was his way to help the community. That explained why they still had her.

Before Vivian had left to return back to their house, she asked me to please keep everything to myself on what we talked about tonight, and when we do talk about Velma, to do it only on our walks, away from the house. "No problem", I replied, as I hugged her goodnight.

After she left I made another pitcher of iced tea for the next day, and went back outside to my rocker. I thought about everything Vivian had said, and it didn't make sense to me at all. Once the sun had set I went inside before the mosquitoes buzzed me, and turned some music on low while I read a book. By ten I was ready to go to bed, and fell into a deep sleep. That was one great thing about living in the country, no noise to keep me awake as it was at the college with the hallway noise, and the car noise from outside my building. There was always noise making it hard to sleep at times. I sure liked not having to deal with it any longer. I loved the peace and quiet around here! It was so tranquil here.

# GENDER REVEAL

My doctor appointment went well, and I was definitely pregnant with a due date in late February. Vivian let out a happy glee of excitement when the doctor came back into the room confirming the results. Drew was smiling from ear to ear. Me, I wasn't sure how I felt. Being told I was pregnant only meant the procedure had worked. I didn't have any feelings of a pregnancy, so in a way it was only words to me. I don't think I will feel pregnant until my belly starts to protrude, or I feel the baby move around a little.

That night we went out to dinner to celebrate the pregnancy news at a really beautiful place on the waterfront. I thought they would come up with a reason to celebrate a meal out as they often do. I was happy for Vivian and Drew to become parents they had always wanted to be. All they could talk about was the baby.

Vivian was hoping for a girl, but in reality she didn't care if it turns out to be a boy. As long as the baby was healthy. Drew agreed with her last comment, as long as it's healthy, as he leaned over and hugged her so sweetly.

I continued to walk nightly around the perimeter of the field for some fresh air, and healthy exercise. It also gave me time to reflect on the day as well as what to expect in the future. Once in awhile both Vivian and Drew would join me on the walk as well, and enjoyed a glass of iced tea afterwards on my back deck. Once Drew started joining us for the iced tea, Vivian had purchased another high back rocking chair so we could all have our own to sit in, and relax.

All summer long I joined them for their grilling on Saturday nights. Many times they invited other people to join them as well, and it was great. They were mostly people that worked for Drew at his law firm, and they were all very kind. Most of the time Vivian's parents and siblings, and all of Drew's family were included with our grilling nights. Vivian parents were very nice, and so happy for them when they announced that they were expecting again. I could tell her sisters weren't as happy as the others, and when I went inside to use the bathroom later, I had overheard them talking about the news. They felt that it shouldn't have even been announced that they were expecting again since they will be grieving in a matter of weeks to come. The older sister agreed wondering how many more times they were going to do this before they realize it was hopeless for Vivian to carry a full term healthy baby.

How sad that was, that her sisters felt that way. All Vivian and Drew wanted was to have a family like they had hoped for, like everyone else had. There wasn't any competition in having kids. It was simple, all they wanted was a family. I quickly made it to the bathroom without being seen, and did my business before returning back to the patio. No one had noticed I had been gone, and I was glad of that as I placed some more strawberries on my plate to eat.

Vivian and I became the best of friends throughout the summer. Many times just sitting on the patio or my deck trying to stay cool. The high humidity, and the heat made the days seem so long. We were glad the nights were cooler, and usually there was a slight breeze felt when we went for our walks. When I went to bed, I left the arcadia door open with the screen locked, so I could get some breeze through the house at night. Drew wanted to purchase a room size air conditioner for me, but I refused telling him I was actually fine. I had never used an air conditioner in the past, so I was accustomed to not having one. He asked me to tell him if it ever got too hot for me though. I agreed that I would.

Summer seemed to have flown by fast. It was the end of summer when Vivian started to wear her fake belly. Velma made several remarks to Vivian about her getting fat. She always seemed to have a knack of saying rude comments. At first it really made Vivian angry, but lately she overlooked Velma's crude remarks. Vivian said Velma had no clue about the secret she was keeping, and the thought of Velma being played was great. Vivian told me how she had to be very careful when she took the belly off, so Velma would never catch on to the deception.

I also had a belly that was protruding now, but not as fast as I thought it should. It was enough to start wearing larger clothes though. We heard the heartbeat at every doctor visit, but on this past doctor visit we had an ultrasound done. The three of us just stared at the images on the screen as the technician rolled the wand around on my belly in amazement. The baby was forming perfectly, and kicking up a storm. I thought I had felt movement before that day, but I wasn't sure if it was the baby, or just gas. Now I knew it was the baby's movements.

Vivian asked if the technician could tell if it was a boy or girl. She looked up asking if we wanted to know. It didn't matter to me, so I let Vivian and Drew decide if they wanted to know. They wanted to know, but they also wanted to hold a gender party with families present, so they asked the technician to tell me when they left the room. The technician had told me it was a little girl.

They would find out at the party on the weekend when everyone was there for the end-of-summer cook out. I knew how happy Vivian would be. Drew would be too, but I think every father wants a son, so I wasn't sure how he was going to react.

I went to the store the following day to purchase everything needed for the gender party. Plenty of pink and blue streamers, balloons, paper plates, table cloths, and other decorations to place around the patio. I saw a huge banner that I knew I had to get that could be personalized with Vivian and Drew's names on it as the proud parents to be.

The bakery had white cupcakes baked and decorated in time with pink centers, and pink and blue frosting on top. Drew had everything they needed for the cookout as far as food went. We made sure not to bother Velma with anything, so she couldn't complain about all the extra work it caused her to do, if she had helped. Velma had been invited, but made an excuse that she had a birthday party she had already said she'd attend. I was rather glad she wouldn't attend anyhow, so it didn't upset me any. Later Vivian had told me she was rather glad Velma wouldn't be coming herself.

When I was busy hanging up the banner, I could see Velma eagle-eye me from the kitchen window. It wasn't two seconds after I was done with the decorations, Velma came outside, and up to me saying she noticed I was getting a little pudgy around my middle myself. She was wondering if I was pregnant, too. That really stumped me for a minute. She laughed, and said she knew it when I didn't answer her right away. I don't see how, I wasn't that big at all. The larger clothes I was wearing weren't revealing a pregnancy by any means. Just like wearing an over-sized top. I told her that I was, and to please not mention it to Vivian or Drew until I had the chance to tell them myself. Boy, her eyes lit up huge with her thinking she knew something she could hold against me. She was so happy she knew something that Vivian and Drew didn't know yet, so she thought. She had such a sly weasel-like smile spread across her face. I quickly dropped the fact I was due in late April, but I wasn't going to keep the baby.

I knew right away she'd spill the beans to Vivian and Drew as soon as she could, but not sure where, when, or how. It definitely was something I needed to warn Vivian and Drew about as soon as I could. They didn't need to be blind-sighted by Velma.

I went to get a bottle of water for myself in the house, and overheard Velma talking on the phone. I stopped since she obviously didn't know I was there to let her continue with her conversation. She was telling the person on the other end of the phone line that she may have found a way to finally get her chance to live in the little house now. Velma had said I had gotten myself knocked up, and just so sure of herself that Drew would kick me out now, and she would be able to finally move in.

She wanted to live in my house badly for some reason. Something was strange about that whole thought process that she had, but I couldn't figure out what, or why. Such a choice of words to use about me… "knocked up". That was hurtful to hear, but then again I considered the source. She had no clue what was going on, but her big mouth rambled on and on.

Drew was outside preparing everything on the grill when his family and Vivian's family started to arrive. They thought everything looked great. I watched for Velma, but so far nothing seemed out of the ordinary with her. I hadn't had the time to tell either Vivian or Drew what happened earlier with Velma's and my little chat. I just hope nothing would be said that night at the gender party before I could warn them myself. I let out a sigh of relief once I saw Velma in her car pulling away from the house.

With Velma gone, I was able to enjoy the food, and the party myself. Vivian and Drew looked radiant as the time for the gender reveal had quickly approached. They grabbed their tubes that they had to pull on, and as we counted down from five. They tugged on their tubes with pink confetti flying out the other ends, and into the air. They were so happy…even Drew. He scooped Vivian up hugging her as he twirled her around. Everyone cheered for them. I looked over to the sisters, and noticed they were smiling as well. Maybe they have accepted the fact Vivian and Drew were having a family this time. I sure hope so.

After everyone left, and we had the place cleaned up, I asked Vivian and Drew if we could talk in the morning. I didn't want to be a downer on their happiness tonight to talk about Velma, but they needed to be aware of what had transpired earlier. They invited me to have breakfast with them at nine, and I agreed.

After we were done with breakfast we drove to the lake which wasn't too far from their house. Sitting at a picnic table under a pavilion I told them of the conversation with Velma. Drew was the first to laugh out loud followed shortly by Vivian. They assured me it worked out perfect for her to find out, and especially when I said I was due two months after "Vivian's due date". I also told them what I had overheard while she was talking on the phone to someone. I didn't mention her remark about me being "knocked up". I decided to keep that to myself since it was their baby I was carrying. Drew assured me that I wouldn't have to leave the house, and there was no way that Velma was ever going to live on their property, period.

I was glad that was in the open now, and also that Velma wasn't getting my place no matter what. In fact, Drew asked me how it was going with me living in the house. I loved living in it. It was so cozy, and the perfect size. That was when he asked if I would like to live there as a renter after the baby was born. I shook my head up and down before my answer of "yes" came out of my mouth. I was thrilled with opportunity to stay there.

It didn't take Velma long to approach Vivian and Drew over my condition. From what Vivian had told me later was that they, Drew and her, played as if they hadn't known anything. Velma wanted to know what they planned to do about it when she told them I was also pregnant. Drew cleared his throat as if he had been caught off guard when he actually had to choke a laugh back. He paused for a few minutes saying he wasn't sure. He was bound by a lease contract for a year, and he wasn't sure what he would do after that. Velma said she thought I had mentioned that there was a clause in my rental contract that only I was to be in the house. Me and only me which didn't count for a baby.

Drew asked Velma what she thought he should do about it. Vivian said she got all smiley saying if I didn't live in the house that she would be more than happy to pay rent, and live there herself so they wouldn't lose any rental money. "Hmm, that's food for thought", Drew had replied, and said he'd have to think about it. Velma left Drew's office thinking she finally had the chance to live in the little house after all, and Velma was determined to get me out somehow or another. I'm sure her evil twisted mind was spinning like a hamster wheel plotting the details on how to get me away from there. What an evil person she was. All about her, all the time to get herself in deeper with Drew and Vivian for some strange reason.

When Vivian and I went on our walk that evening she was telling me all this. She remarked that Velma had known something only Drew and her had discussed in the house during the week. Velma had let it slip out, and before she could catch herself she put it on to Vivian by asking, "Wasn't that what you had told me the other day"? Vivian knew she never discussed it with her, and it made Drew and Vivian both suspicious on how Velma found that bit of information.

Vivian said it was concerning her side of the family, and she hadn't told me anything about it yet, so she knew I couldn't have told Velma. I assured her that I speak as little as possible to Velma, and would never tell her personal things that Vivian tells me. What she tells me stays with me, so she didn't have to worry about me spilling any beans. It sure was strange how Velma seemed to know about things that had been said only between them. Could Velma actually be clairvoyant after all? I found that hard to believe because if she was clairvoyant, she'd know more than just a few things. Like the baby

I'm carrying, Vivian's fake belly, and so on. It had to be some other reason. Something we're overlooking. I just didn't know what, but I was going to keep my ears and eyes open, and watch what I say so Velma could never find out what was going on between Drew, Vivian, and myself that she could use to do damage anything that her evil mind could think of.

# My Best Friend's Husband

# $\mathcal{B}$UGS

Since the gender party, Vivian and I have gone shopping for baby items almost weekly. This baby is going to be very well dressed, and have everything possible to play with. Drew reminded Vivian that there was going to be a baby shower in January which people will be buying outfits, and items as well, so not to go so crazy now. I could tell Vivian was excited, and I hated to ruin her fun shopping, but I knew Drew was right.

My appointments were going great. We'd listen to the heartbeat each visit, and the doctor complimented me on my weight being exceptionally great. I was feeling great. I didn't have the morning sickness I thought I would have at all, little heartburn now and then, and I still had a pep of energy every day. The baby was doing great, too. That was the most important factor to all of us.

I was feeling her kicks more frequently now, as she was a very active little one. Vivian asked if I minded if she could feel the kicks on my belly one night. I didn't have a problem with that. It was rewarding to see her face light up when she felt the kicks from her daughter. One weekend when we knew no one else was at home, and she wasn't wearing her fake belly, I asked if she would stand in front of me. I let my belly touch her belly when the baby was kicking through our shirts so she was able to sense what it was like to feel the kicks on her stomach herself. She was beyond happy to know what it was like to have her little girl kick her stomach. When I saw tears in her eyes, I knew she was feeling something she never would have probably felt ever, and I was glad to let her feel the movements for as long as she wanted. It made her day. As soon as Drew came home she told him about it. He was pleased I had allowed Vivian the chance to feel true kicks like that on her own belly.

October was upon us, and the nights were chillier than normal. I had to bundle up when I went for my walks. The leaves were so vibrant of color, and the crispness in the air felt good. It was so beautiful all around. Country living was the best as far as I was concerned.

My job at the dentist office had changed from receptionist to doing the bookkeeping. I was very happy about that because I was able to work from home four of the five days part time. I went in on Friday afternoons to gather all the necessary paperwork I needed, and took it home with me. The dentist was very pleased with the work I had been doing on the bookkeeping, and offered to bring me the paperwork once it started to snow, so I wouldn't have to be out on the snowy roads in my condition. I was glad to stay off the roads as each week passed with my belly getting large enough to rub against the steering wheel. It also saved me from the office gossip, questions, and the drama going on in the office.

Vivian and I had made up plenty of treat bags for the kids that will be coming around on Halloween night. Velma made her opinion known that she thought it was foolish to go to all the extra trouble, saying the kids could careless about how the bags look. They just want the candy. I was enjoying myself making them, and I knew Vivian was also. When I asked if she would like to help, she glared at me as if I had stuffed a sour lemon in her mouth. She hurried out of the room after she grumbled something under her breath, and that she was leaving to go home. I wished her a good weekend, and she just walked past me and was out the door without a response. Go figure!!

The next day Drew helped Vivian decorate the outside of the house for Halloween. They went overboard on everything, but it sure looked great. I knew it was a waste for me to decorate the outside of my place since no one would be going back there. I had a few items decorating the inside of my place, but that was it. Just enough to make it a seasonal festive.

I was at their house to help pass out the bags when the kids came to the door to get their treats, and they seemed so happy with the treat bags Vivian and I had packed full of special treats. It has been so long since I was a kid doing this same thing. Once I was in second grade I wasn't permitted to go out again, and had to stay in my room during the whole candy passing out time. My mother and new stepfather didn't pass out any candy at all. They kept all the lights off while they watched the TV in their room while drinking beer. It was almost the same thing at Thanksgiving. No special meal to give thanks over, but they kept the lights on watching a stupid football game. Such cheerful people I lived with.

When Vivian was talking about the meal that would be prepared for their Thanksgiving dinner in a few days with everyone at the house, I felt a little jealous. Her side of the family, and Drew's side would fill the chairs around the table enjoying a feast that day as one big happy family. It will be just another ordinary day for me. Even Velma had the entire week off to be with her family. Family! I wondered when I will ever have a family of my own to celebrate like this as I walked back to my house that night. I didn't even wait for Drew to walk me home, I just wanted to be by myself to sulk on my own. I wasn't even a few feet from their house when I heard Drew come out the door. He yelled for me to wait up. He didn't want to me slip or fall on my way back to my house.

He could tell right away I was a little upset. He asked if I was okay, and I put a fake smile on saying sure. But I wasn't. When we got to my door he asked if he could come in to talk with me. Good grief, I just wanted to be left alone, but I allowed him to come in. As he sat on the couch he just wanted to tell me how happy I have made them, and how excited they were about their baby doing so well. They have never been as happy at expecting a baby as they have been this year, and it was all because of me.

I smiled because that showed I was appreciated by them, and offered him a cup of herbal tea. As we sat there sipping on the steamy hot tea I felt the baby kick the daylights out of me. Drew noticed my top bouncing around, and asked if it was the baby kicking. I chuckled saying she sure was, and before I thought anything more, I asked if he'd like to feel it moving around.

At first he was hesitant, but I told him it would be fine. He gently placed his hand on my belly, and I held it there firmly. I knew immediately when she kicked. Drew's face lit up, and this huge smile formed on his face. He was pretty stoked to be able to feel his daughter moving around, and feeling her kicks like that. He didn't move his hand, and she kicked several more times. He thanked me for allowing him to feel his daughter's movements. I smiled telling him most fathers have that opportunity, but with the situation the way it was for us, he might have never got the chance to feel them. He thanked me several times before he finally stood up to leave. He said he hoped both of us would bring a good appetite for Thanksgiving dinner.

I must have looked so dumbfounded, and he asked if I was coming. I said I hadn't been invited. He put his hands on my shoulders saying the whole family will be there, and that included me. I was part of their family, and would always be a part of it. I thanked him, gave him a big hug for clarifying where I stood, and said I will be sure to have a healthy appetite then, after all, I was eating for two! He left to go back to his house, and I no longer needed to sulk. I am family.

The next morning I was in a great mood, and thought I'd do some late fall cleaning. A good hard cleaning that I hadn't done in a few weeks. I started in my bedroom with the dusting of the furniture. I hit the lamp shade a little harder than normal, and noticed that something fell off. I looked for it on the end table, but there wasn't anything there. I continued dusting, and started the vacuum sweeper. I as I went under the bed I heard a ping noise like the vacuum had sucked something up other than dust. I quickly turned it off, and took the canister off the vacuum to sift through the dirt to see if I could find it. I found a little metal disc with two little antennae-like things sticking out from it. I checked the lamp to be sure I hadn't broken it, but it worked fine. Nothing seemed missing on it so I threw that dirt away from the vacuum. I did keep the thing I found, and decided I'd ask Drew about it at a later time. I had no clue what it could be.

I told Vivian about it, and she said to bring it with me when I come up for Thanksgiving dinner. I knew it was some sort of electronic device, but not exactly what it could be. It was snowing hard Thanksgiving Day, and everyone was running late getting to the house. Vivian said Drew would come down to get me because the snow was deep already. When he got to the door I remembered that little thing the vacuum had sucked up, so I went to get it. I told him how and where I found it when I handed it to him. He turned it over several times asking if I had any others. I shook my head no, asking what it was. He said he'd tell me outside as we were walking up to the house. I grabbed my coat putting it on with Drew's help, and we were on our way to dinner. Half way there I asked what he thought it was. He said he wasn't sure, but knew that his father would know. That was no help to me!

After everyone finally arrived, and we had dinner, Drew had asked me, Vivian, and his father to come to the basement with him. Drew took the metal item out of his pocket asking his dad if he has ever seen anything like that before. His dad said he had, and asked where it came from. I told him it was in my bedroom lamp shade. He held his finger to his mouth as to shush me right after that. He put it on the floor stomping on it with his heavy boot until it broke into several small pieces. What the heck! He turned to Drew quietly saying we needed to see if there were anymore of them in the house, and in Drew's house as well. It was a listening device known as a bug. I looked at him and said, "bug"? He felt we would probably find others in the house if we looked around, but he had a friend on the police force that he'd call in the morning. He has a hand held device that will detect if there were any other ones present. But, in the meantime not to talk about it, or anything personal in either of the houses, until his friend comes out. Talk about putting a damper on Thanksgiving.

When we went back upstairs everyone wanted to know what was going on. Drew wrote on a piece of paper that I found a listening device in my house. There might be others in the house, and we didn't know who could be listening in on us even now. We passed that paper around for all the adults to read, and they were shocked. Drew's mom was the one who wrote me a note asking if I was okay, and have I ever talked about personal things inside the house. I shook my head no, and she hugged me. We continued on with the rest of the evening as if we didn't know anything about it. Just super careful on what we did say.

That night when Drew and Vivian walked me back to my place after everyone else left, they asked if I felt unsafe staying in there. I was okay. For all we know, it could have been in the lamp since I moved in, and if it was to get information off me, they didn't get anything all this time anyhow. We will know on Monday or Tuesday if there are anymore in either of the houses. I could tell Drew was mad, as he said he would get to the bottom of it.

~

That night when I was laying down to go to sleep it occurred to me that was probably how Velma knew about the movies Drew and Vivian had watched, and the other things we thought were coincidences, or Velma being clairvoyant. It made sense now. It was a good thing we never spoke about our pregnancy in either house, or all the plans that were put in place. I just hope if it was Velma that she didn't hear us talking about finding that bug. With those thoughts out of my head, I finally fell into a nice deep sleep.

We didn't have to wait until Monday or Tuesday for

Drew's father's friend to show up at the house with Drew's dad. They both arrived early on Saturday morning with that hand held device to see if there were anymore bugs. They started first in my house finding three more of them. Talk about invasion of privacy.

We walked to the main house with Drew's dad hanging on to me in case I fell trudging through the snow. In there, they found a total of ten scattered around their house, including in their bedroom. They were hidden very well, and all the same brand. Vivian jotted down where each one was located to keep as a reference. I chuckled saying I wouldn't be surprised if they found one in our cars as well. Officer Pete hadn't checked the cars, but he was more than happy to check after I said that. Low and behold, he found one in all three vehicles as well. Whoever this person was didn't leave anything out in trying to find any information. Vivian and I both knew it had to have been Velma placing them in the houses and cars.

Officer Pete had an extra device in his cruiser, and said he would loan it to us. He said many times when the bugs are found and removed, the person or people involved with them will reinstall more, but in other locations if they were that desperate to obtain information. Drew asked Officer Peter what he could do at this point which Officer Pete had said to be vigilante on what we talk about in the house, and in the vehicles. Anything we felt was personal, or private information shouldn't be discussed in those areas. All of Drew's conversations about, and to clients, needed to be done only in his office from now on. He felt that the culprit will surface some time when we least expect it. That was when we could go after them legally.

On that note, he asked Drew if there was any cases he was working on that might be of concern. Drew stated that he will be having one come up soon, but it was several months down the road yet. Like about a year to be exact, so Drew ruled that out immediately, even though it was a nasty case. In short, Drew had to defend a man years ago, which had sent him to prison for several years, but Drew didn't think that had anything to do with what was going on in his house now. Drew and Officer Pete were stumped on who it might be, but Officer Pete left with his verbal reminder to be vigilante, and to sweep the houses weekly or so with the bug detector he had left with Drew.

With that excitement over for the day, the three of us decided to go to lunch. Drew's dad and Officer Pete had been invited along as well. After lunch Vivian and I had gone shopping for Christmas gifts. I had drawn Drew's mother for our gift exchange. She wrote several items down that she would like, so it was easy for me to find her something. Since I only had three people to buy for I was done in no time, so I went to the book store finding a few books for myself after scanning all the new arrivals. The weather was keeping me inside most days, and I'm not much of a TV watcher, so I needed something to occupy myself. Work kept me busy during the day, but it was the long nights that I was bored with. The roads were pretty good when we got to the cafe, but after shopping, on the way home it started to snow making it slippery. Drew took it easy by slowing down, and being extra careful getting us home safe.

Vivian had me stay for dinner consisting of grilled cheese sandwiches, and tomato soup. It was fast, easy, and warmed us up on this dreary day. Afterwards we played cards for awhile, and then Drew walked me home waiting patiently until I was in my house before he turned to walk back to his house. I feel so fortunate having them as friends. More than friends, they're my family.

# Baby Time

With the snow being as high as it was, and the temperatures being so low, I didn't venture outside very often. I mostly worked on the billings for the dentist, and sent out reminders of upcoming appointments by email. There were days I whizzed though everything which left me without anything else to do the rest of the day. Vivian came down several days in the week to keep me company. She would always bring the bug detector with her, and we would scan the rooms before we started talking. Even after sweeping the house with the detector, we weren't one hundred per cent sure if it worked right. Officer Pete had said if we absolutely needed to talk, to turn on the radio or something to drown us out from being heard, so we did that that as a precautionary measure to keep from being heard.

Vivian was sure as heck positive that it was Velma trying to get information to use against us, or about Drew and her. Vivian said there has been a guy calling once in a while to speak to Velma. Velma always walked out of the room when she spoke with the man on the phone, so Vivian had no idea who it could be. Wonder why he didn't call her on her cell phone!!

Maybe Velma had a new man in her life, but she never shared any details with us. Vivian didn't trust Velma with anything. She couldn't explain why, but it was a gut feeling she had that Velma was bad news. Velma started working for them from an agency that match up people for Drew's project, and said she was highly recommended, and that her previous employer was happy with her work however, that was over ten years ago before she had quit working, and started stealing for money. Bet they never had their house bugged, I'm sure!

Velma was going to be gone again during Christmas week to be with her family. The three of us were going to Drew's parents house two hours away to celebrate the holiday there. Everyone was going to be there like they were at Thanksgiving. We decided to leave right after my checkup at the doctors that Friday afternoon.

I have been going to the doctors every two weeks now, and I have to admit, I was feeling uncomfortable lately. The doctor said that was normal, and it would be over soon. Just to continue what I have been doing, and to stay off my feet more often during the day. It would help with the swelling in my feet. Drew and Vivian saw the baby moving around when the doctor was checking me. They have felt her movement often, and were ecstatic each time. The doctor thought that was really good for them to feel her movement to build a bond with their baby, and with the pregnancy.

Christmas was very nice, and everyone was happy with their gifts. Drew had drawn my name. He gave me the most beautiful heart shaped pendant with a nice size diamond in the middle. On the back side he had it engraved, "Family Forever". He hugged me, and thanked me once again for being a part of their lives. He also whispered for making it possible for Vivian and him to have a baby. I smiled thanking him adding "for everything".

Later that night when I was in bed I thought how lucky I was to have answered the ad they had placed in the newspaper that week. Not only was I able to pay my student loan off, I lived rent free in a very nice house, have them for great friends, and have saved so much money from my job to live a better life style once my contract is over.

Better news yet, there was a big surprise I received in the mail a few weeks back. It was a check for the entire amount of money I had paid the college in order to receive my degree. Vivian had told Drew about it after we were talking about what I had spent the first installment of the contract money on. (I didn't tell them I had planned on buying a large savings bond for the baby once she was born). Drew had pursued and retrieved my money on his own, and saw that the college was completely wrong in charging me like they had. He told them they had taken advantage of me. He was willing to go the whole distance it would take for me to get every single penny back with interest occurred during that time. I couldn't thank them enough for doing that for me.

Vivian had asked me to go with them to a New Years celebration the following day, but I declined. I was feeling pretty miserable, and my feet kept swelling to elephant size no matter how much I had them propped up. I figured they needed a night out by themselves before the baby would arrive. I was sound asleep when the New Year rang in, but later that night I was woken up by something scratching on the side of my house. There weren't any branches hanging over the house, so I figured it had to have been an animal, at least I hoped so. I watched outside my arcadia door for about a half hour, and low and behold, a deer had walked out. It must have wanted to shelter itself out of the brutal wind. I was glad that it had been a deer. Since this whole thing on finding the bugs in our houses had left me feeling uneasy at times.

Vivian's baby shower was held later in January by her mother and sisters. I wasn't sure if I should attend, but Vivian insisted on me being there with her. She felt like the baby shower was for the both of us since I was the one carrying their baby. It was at the shower that Vivian announced that they were naming their baby Avery Sam. Everyone liked the name Avery, but they couldn't figure out why Sam until Vivian explained that Sam were the initials of her mother and Drew's mother's middle name, and the grandmother she had always been very close with. Everyone thought that was a beautiful name then.

We were seeing the doctor every week now, and he informed us the baby had already turned getting into the delivery stage of birth. He didn't think I would make it to the due date, so we needed to get ourselves prepared for her arrival.

The doctor thought I probably better not walk on the treadmill any longer in case I should happen to fall. I have used that treadmill every single day since the weather got bad, but I could understand his concern. I had it in the basement, which he was also concerned about me falling on the stairs as well. Well, I decided I'd just walk from one end of my house to the other to get the exercise I needed.

It wasn't three weeks later that I started to get a bad backache, and it was nothing like previous backaches I have ever had. No matter how I would sit, or lay on the bed, it made its presence known. I had wondered if I was having the beginning stages of labor pains, so I called the nurse help line to ask. She suggested that I get checked by my doctor as soon as I could. Great! I called Vivian to ask if she could take me to the doctor's office. She was down to my house within minutes to pick me up. It felt like hours before we finally got to the doctor's office. He checked me over saying I needed to go immediately to the hospital, and he would be right over in a few minutes. I was definitely in labor, and was dilated at a seven. I couldn't believe it. I thought I would have an enormous amount of pain. Vivian called Drew telling him to meet us at the hospital right away because their daughter was getting close to being born.

I was taken right into a room to change into a hospital gown, and be checked by the nurse. The doctor had called the hospital already telling the nurses to get me prepped as soon as they could. Once the doctor arrived, I was wheeled into the delivery room, and was already on the delivery table when Vivian and Drew came in gowned up. They came over to wish me the best, and giving me a hug before they went to the wall to wait.

∼

I told the nurses that they were my coaches, and I needed them by my side. The doctor nodded that it was okay. They both held my hands giving me great encouragement when the pain started to make its presence known. Before I knew it the pain had subsided, and I heard a little cry from the baby. Vivian and Drew were so happy. They both hugged and kissed my checks. The nurse cleaned her up as much as she needed, and was bringing her over to me to hold. I stopped the nurse telling her to let Vivian and Drew hold her first. They were her parents, and I felt they should be the ones to hold her before me. Vivian was crying tears of joy so much when she was handed her little daughter. Drew was standing right behind Vivian holding Avery's little hand. I could see his misty eyes as they kissed their baby before they handed her to me.

She was a beautiful baby, perfect coloring, head full of dark brown hair, and the most angelic face I had ever seen on a newborn. I didn't hold back those thoughts when I handed her back to Vivian either because she was that beautiful. Finally the nurse had to take her back to weigh, measure, and get a blood test. Before Vivian and Drew left they came over thanking me once again. Vivian was crying when she whispered that I was the one who made this happen for them, and they would love me for the rest of their lives. Drew also thanked me by telling me that this was the happiest day of their lives. I couldn't believe it was over already. The doctor finished what he had to do, and before I knew it I was being rolled to another room.

I had been moved to a room clear down the hall from all the other mothers, and the nursery. I didn't understand why I wasn't with the rest of the new mothers. This isn't where the doctor had said I'd be after delivery. I didn't care at the moment as I was pretty tired, and shortly fell asleep.

When I woke up later, I could hear voices in the hallway. Drew was arguing with the nurse at the desk that I did not belong by myself away from all the other mothers. Drew must have made the nurse angry because she spouted out to him that the ones who give their babies away aren't to be with those who have kept their babies. Did that ever anger Drew!! Drew slammed something down on the desk while yelling something back to her. The next thing I heard was her telling him that she was going to call security if he didn't leave. Knowing Drew as I have learned, he wouldn't let this slide, and I was right.

It wasn't an hour later when the nurse came in to move me closer to the nursery, and closer to Vivian. Drew had gone to the head of the nurses to file a complaint, and threat of a lawsuit if I wasn't removed from where they had tucked me away. Drew had paid for a room for Vivian and him to stay in during the time. They were going to be there with Avery, and he wanted me as close to that room as possible. That had been arranged with our doctor to have it that way, and Drew was going to be calling the doctor himself to let him know what that nurse had done and had said.

That nurse refused to have anything to do with me after that, and I really didn't care. She had a bad attitude towards me for some reason right from the beginning, and I hadn't done anything wrong. Vivian and Drew had a dozen beautiful pink roses delivered to my adjoining room with a thank you card. I heard that nurse talking about me receiving them saying I had no shame by giving away my baby, and yet receive some flowers. Well, she said that to the wrong person, and I know Drew heard it as well because he stormed out of their room going straight to the nurse's station. He called the head of the nurses once again, and wanted her to come to their room immediately. Once he told her what nurse PJ had said, I could hear PJ being called to their room...stat. Once everything had been brought out in the open, and confirmed to be true, PJ had to get her things, and leave until further notice.

I didn't want to stir up problems, but Vivian and Drew were protecting me from dealing with PJ and her nasty comments. I rolled over in my bed softly crying before falling asleep. When I woke up Vivian, Drew, and little Avery were coming into my room for a visit. Vivian handed Avery to me to hold her once again. She was so precious. It was her feeding time, and I had the pleasure of feeding her. My heart melted. I asked what her weight, and length was at birth. They said she was seven pounds even, and twenty inches long. I gazed into her little eyes wondering if she would ever understand how she actually became a daughter to her mom and dad when she got older. She was their little miracle, and it gave me great pleasure to be a part of it.

Vivian said they were having her baptized in four weeks, and asked me to be Avery's Godmother. I accepted that honor immediately knowing Avery would always be a part of my life. I had to hurry, and get out of this place now. I had to help with the baptism, and had to shop for her baptismal gown. Believe you me, I was going to pick the prettiest one out, no matter the cost. This was a special time for everyone, but it was extra special for me in more ways than I care to think about.

Drew drove me home before Vivian and Avery so no one would be the wiser when they would arrive home with Avery. Vivian had the bellies in a tub for me in my basement to use for the next five to six weeks to keep the charade going for a little longer. About an hour after he dropped me off at my little house, I saw Vivian and Drew's parents arrive to greet their little granddaughter once they arrived home. The excitement they had to have for Avery was pure happiness. I was happy for them.

As time went on I was there to watch Avery grow, to do all the wonder things expected of her from rolling over, to crawling, and eventually pulling herself upright all before her first birthday. She was a very happy and content baby, and I can't say it enough, what a great mother Vivian was with her. You could see both Vivian and Drew beam with happiness over Avery. That was such a comfort knowing they were great parents. I was invited along on many outings with them. Some I accepted, but there were times when I felt they didn't really need me tagging along as they did something special together as a family. I had the pleasure of watching Avery for Vivian and Drew to have a date night every few weeks.

Velma was very angry when Drew decided he was going to rent the house to me that she had desperately wanted to live in. She gave me the most disgusted looks when I was at the house, and complained that I made myself at home there too soon, by going to the refrigerator to get things whenever I wanted. Drew told Velma it had been his decision on me staying, and I had been told to help myself when I was there so she wouldn't be put out having to wait on me. I guess that sent her over the edge, and she brought up several things she didn't like about me. Drew told her to calm down, and either she would go by his rules and expectations, or she could give notice to leave. That calmed her down quickly, and she decided to shut her mouth so she could stay.

Vivian and I were back to walking the perimeter of the

field with Avery in her stroller or in the sling that Vivian had to carry her in. That was the only time we felt safe to talk openly. Vivian told me things that she had caught Velma doing, like going through papers in Drew's office desk as if she was searching for something. Drew was very careful on what he left at the house because of that reason alone. They didn't know what she was trying to find, but it must have been very important to her.

Everything was going great for me. I worked my mornings for the dentist then had the rest of the day free. I continued to use my treadmill several days during the week when I didn't feel like walking the field alone. Once in a while I would feel unsafe walking it, and didn't want to take that chance of throwing caution to the wind, too.

Shortly after Avery turned two years old Drew had asked if I could come to the office downtown for a meeting. I had no idea why I needed to come to his office, but I told him to name the time and day, and I would be there. I felt it must be very important seeing that he wanted it at his downtown office when we could have met at the home.

When I arrived at the office, I saw Vivian's car in the parking lot. I couldn't imagine what was going on. Drew called me into his office, and there was Vivian with Avery as well. First thing that came to my mind was that they wanted me to move out of their small house. Drew looked so serious as he started talking. He was directing all his comments about Avery, and how happy I had made them, what a beautiful baby she was and such. Vivian couldn't stand the drawn out comments. She finally blurted out that they wanted another baby, and if I would be willing to do it again for them. Another baby! They felt I had done a great job carrying Avery for them, and they wanted to ask me first before they went any further with the notion of enlarging their family.

They were planning on doing the same contract as before, if I agreed to do it again. I hadn't thought of doing it again, but I also saw how much happiness it had brought into their lives with Avery. They were very pleased with how I took care of myself while carrying their baby, allowing them to feel Avery kicking, and able to keep the pregnancy secret. I didn't have to think about it very long. Before I left the office I had signed another contract.

Was I doing the right thing? I knew I was. I was very happy with everything before, so I couldn't see any reason not to do it again. We were family, and I saw how happy Drew and Vivian were as a family, and how well they have always treated me. So, here I go again….

# LOSS OF LIFE

It wasn't long after being impregnated once again, I knew it had worked. I was feeling great most of the time, but was experiencing a little more morning sickness this time than before with Avery. One afternoon I met Vivian on her patio for some talk time. Avery was busy in the enclosed area with several toys to play with while we talked. It was such a beautiful day until Velma came outside. Velma acted like she was cleaning something when we knew she was there to only to eavesdrop on our conversation.

Drew set the appointment up with the doctor to confirm if the procedure had worked. Once it was confirmed it had, a big bar-b-que was set for the following Saturday to announce it to the family that they were expecting once again. Drew would grill as usual, and bring all the steaks inside to eat since it was still snowy, and cold outside. They weren't waiting any longer this time to let the family know their news. First thing Velma said when she heard the news was that she was there to clean the house, and for them not to expect her to watch any kids. She wasn't a babysitter or a nanny. In fact, she didn't really like kids at all. They were too noisy and messy as far as she was concerned. Vivian calmly told her they would keep that in mind as time gets closer. Vivian turned to me rolling her eyes, and whispered "witch".

Once everyone was settled at the dining room table chowing down on the delicious meal Drew had grilled, he and Vivian made their announcement of having another baby. Her sisters were sitting close to me, and I could see their mouths drop open in shock. The oldest sister mouthed to the other, "why"? Of course their parents were very happy for them by congratulating them immediately.

Later, I overheard the two sisters say they couldn't understand why Vivian and Drew would want to even try for another baby. That they both should be happy with the one they already have, and leave it that way. I couldn't believe how cynical they were towards their own sister, and her happiness. Vivian had told me in the past that she was never close to them. She never understood what she had done to cause the riff between the three of them, so she had decided to stay at a distance, be nice when she had to, but not be overly friendly. I could see why Vivian felt that way now. A few times I had overheard them make comments that I thought weren't nice, but I kept them to myself. Vivian was my best friend, and they were her family, her blood family.

A few days later Vivian came down to the house to go for a walk with me. Drew was watching Avery at the house. I knew it had to be something important for her not to be bringing Avery with her. She wanted me to know that Drew was working on something important that she was very concerned about. It was to be kept very quiet. I assured her I wouldn't say a word. Vivian should know I don't have other friends other than her and Drew that I socialize with, but maybe she was referring to the rest of the family. Either way, I don't spill the beans on what I have seen or have been told.

Apparently a few years ago Drew was representing a client on charges of embezzlement from the company he had worked for. Drew had lost the case, and the client was sent to prison for ten years. Drew knew from the beginning it was an open and shut case, but he took it doing his best for his client.

The state had done their job, and the evidence was overwhelming with the guy being convicted. When the jurors came back with a guilty verdict, the guy had vowed to get even with Drew when he got out of prison. He will be getting out in about a year now, and Drew is concerned what the client may do to him. I was really surprised with that information being shared with me. The way Drew had handled everything in the hospital over my room situation, and my tuition from college, I had felt he was a very powerful man, and no one ever threatened him like that. Vivian was worried what that client was capable of, and how far he would go to get "even". Maybe after being in prison he realized it wouldn't have mattered who had defended him, he would have been found guilty, and there was no reason for him to carry out his threats to Drew.

Vivian was worried about herself and Avery as well. It was worrying Vivian to the extreme that she started losing sleep from the worry. Every noise she heard in or outside the house she thought it could be that client, even though she knew he was still in prison behind bars. She was worried about anything and everything which was driving her completely crazy. She couldn't even go to the store alone anymore in fear that something might happen to her or Avery then. And she was losing hair by the handful over this worry.

I felt so bad for her, but I could see that she was overboard on the fear she was experiencing. I was a good listener letting her get it all out of her system in hopes it would be of some comfort. I assured her that I understood, and if she wanted me to go with her anywhere I would be more than happy to. She thought maybe the doctor could give her something to help her, but she was worried what if it didn't help, or it made things worse. I told her I'd watch Avery at my place if she wanted to see the doctor. (I just didn't want to be in the same house as Velma). Vivian agreed to make the appointment, and I'd watch Avery for her. She didn't want anyone to know that she was feeling this way, and I promised her I wouldn't say a word.

I watched Avery the next afternoon when Vivian went

to the doctors. He prescribed a medication for her anxiety that he said she was experiencing. I think just talking to the doctor helped her as she was in better spirits when she came to pick Avery up. I was glad of that. I hated to see Vivian so upset. But, we also knew that there was something else happening that neither of us were aware of. Whatever it was was, we just couldn't put our finger on it.

I was finally far enough along in the pregnancy to have an ultrasound done. We were having another baby girl. Vivian was all smiles. Drew smiled, but I think he was really hoping for a boy this time. Maybe he had too much on his mind to think about anything else with that case he was working on. Vivian already had names picked out for the baby. Ansley Sue for a girl, and the same name for the boy as before, Andrew James Williamson II, if it had been a boy. I was honored with the middle name of the girl being the same as mine. Vivian had planned it that way using my middle name, and wanted the names to be known from the start. As we left the doctor's office Vivian grabbed my arm stating she felt funny. We stopped for her to catch her breath before we continued to our cars. After Avery was secured in her car seat we went home. Drew had some more work to do at the office, and would be home later.

Another girl! I was happy with that. I would have been happy if it had been a boy as well. Vivian had kept all of Avery's clothes, so there wasn't much Vivian would need for Ansley. I saw how tired Drew had been the past few nights when we were at the doctor's office. Bags were developing under his eyes, and dark circles around them. I could tell he wasn't getting the sleep he needed. This case he was working on was getting to him as well. And he was probably worried over Vivian and Avery, too. Also with another baby on the way was about all he needed at that time. I decided I needed to look into this case myself to see what has everyone so upset over. I just needed to get the name of the client to search for on the internet. Maybe Vivian will let me know, and if not, I will look for newspaper clippings, and articles around that time frame. I will find out one way or another.

## Present time

I couldn't put any of this right in my head. When I heard all the sirens, and the commotion going on at the house I quickly got dressed to see what was happening. Vivian's parents drove into the driveway as if her father was driving in the Indy 500. Once they got out of their car they literally ran into the house. My first thought was that something had happened to Avery, and my stomach was in knots from that thought. I walked up to the house as fast as I could to see if everything was okay. Drew sat on the couch in a heap of a mess holding onto Avery. Vivian's mom took Avery from him, and I knew then, it had to have been Vivian.

Vivian had passed away in her sleep during the night. **NO!!!** I just didn't hear that. That just couldn't have happened. I got weak in the knees, and had to sit down immediately. I could not believe this shocking news. So many thoughts raced through my mind. Poor Vivian who was so happy, and now she was gone. I just sat there. The feeling in my body had drained away, and I couldn't move. Someone was talking to me, I think. I could see their lips move, but heard no sound. They think as of right now that Vivian had a heart attack. I thought about the pills she had been taking to calm her anxiety. Was everything too much for her? Did she accidentally take one pill too many? Should I say something about the pills, or should I just not say anything about them. I had promised Vivian I wouldn't tell anyone about the pills the day she started taking them. The police were talking to everyone, and I expected them to talk with me soon enough.

Trying to cope with the news had left me so devastated. I had never had such a best friend my entire life until I met Vivian. She helped me through so many obstacles I had, as well as confiding with me on things she was dealing with herself that she felt sure no one would take her serious nor understand. And now she was gone. My best friend was gone. I just sat there at the kitchen counter watching as the police walked around the place. I couldn't cry a single tear. Just the devastation across Drew's face was enough to make me want to scream. This couldn't be right. Something wasn't right. Vivian couldn't be dead. We had talked just last night, and she was feeling happy. She had just put Avery to bed, and after she drank a cup of tea she was going to bed herself. Someone please help me understand!!

I needed air. I stood up and started to leave when

Drew's mother came over to me, and hugged me. She saw me alone with a look of sadness and shock across my face. She knew I needed to be comforted. That was when I cried, and I cried hard into her shoulder. That was just about the time when Avery started crying loudly for her mommy. She didn't want her grandmother to hold her, and was trying to squirm out of her arms. As soon as she saw me she held out her hands for me, and calling "Ali Ali". I quickly went to her, and told Vivian's mom, that I'd take her to my place away from all this commotion. It was hard enough on all of us, and I know Avery must have been confused to why everyone was crying, and with so many other strangers in her house. I fed Avery some breakfast, and held her until she fell asleep rocking her in my rocking chair. The poor little girl was now without a mommy to help her with everything. Avery would be feeling the loss of her mommy soon enough, and will wonder where she is when this happens. It is such a tragic shame for the family, and also for Vivian not being able to watch her daughters grow up. **Daughters**. Oh my, I was carrying another daughter for Vivian that she will never feel kicking inside me, or be there as Ansley hits all the milestones babies do while growing up. Just as I was putting Avery on my bed to sleep, the police officers knocked on my door to talk to me. They didn't ask anything about Vivian's pills for anxiety. They were mostly concerned if Vivian had mentioned to me about being threatened by anyone, or if I knew if there was someone that Vivian was concerned about on hurting her, or the baby. I told them the only thing I could think of was the case that her husband was working on. They asked if that was about the Joshua Jones case? I replied that I didn't know what his name was, which I didn't, until now. They thanked me handing me their cards if I should remember something, to give them a call.

～

Shortly Drew's mom came to see how I was, and how Avery was doing. She saw her on my bed asleep saying she'd come by later to get her, if I didn't mind watching her longer. There was so much that had to be done yet in making the arrangements, and Drew wasn't of much help yet. He was still dealing with the shock that his wife was gone. I asked Mrs. Williamson if there was anything I could help with. She couldn't think of anything at the moment. I offered the fact the Vivian and Drew had funeral plans wrote out somewhere in the safe, if that was of any help. I had been told about that when I first signed on the dotted line to get pregnant for Avery. That was the only place I thought they might need to look. She thanked me, and asked me to please call her Carolyn before she headed back to the main house.

It was rather late that night before anyone came back to my house. This time it was Drew. He looked a mess, and it looked like he had aged twenty years since last night. I gave him a hug telling him how sorry I was. I couldn't hold the tears back. Drew couldn't either as he hugged me hard. He was able to tell me they were doing an autopsy in the morning, but it looked like a heart attack as of now. They set the funeral for Saturday so other family members could make it to town in time to be there. Drew thanked me for telling his mom about the papers in the safe. Vivian was pretty organized, and very detailed on what she wanted in her funeral. They had purchased several lots at a cemetery when they wrote their will, which was where Vivian was going to be laid to rest. Then in June when the weather was nice they would have a private celebration of life on the patio with the family. I asked if I could please say something at her funeral, and he said he knew that Vivian would like that. I felt I had to say something for what she meant to me. After another hug from Drew, he picked Avery up into his arms, and went back to their house.

Many people attended Vivian's funeral to give their condolences that Saturday. I had written out my eulogy, and as I was reading it, I could feel Vivian's presence next to me. A special calmness came over me. It was a wonderful feeling. I knew then, Vivian would always be with me. After everything was over, we were invited back to the house for lunch. Drew searched me out among all the people there to tell me what a beautiful eulogy I had written. He was able to tell how much Vivian had meant to me. Drew said I had meant a lot to Vivian as well, and thanked me. He knew Vivian was closer to me than to her sisters, and he was happy she had me for a friend that she could always rely on. He hugged me before he returned to his other guests.

That night I had a hard time falling asleep thinking of Vivian, and everything we had shared. I wasn't sure where I was in the family picture anymore though. I was carrying their baby, and nothing had been mentioned to me about what was going to happen now. I wondered if Drew would even want to raise a newborn baby by himself. What were the plans now? One thought after another wandered through my head, and then it hit me. I sat up in bed so fast grabbing my laptop computer I almost fell onto the floor. I have the name of the client that Vivian was telling me about now, and I was going to do some research on him. I was sure Vivian would have wanted me to.

I typed in the name the police officer had said, Joshua Jones, along with the state. Wow! There was so much information about him that I could see why Vivian was concerned now. This guy was really bad news. In fact, the article said he was a "mean and dangerous hombre" and had other problems in his past that they couldn't bring up in court. The company he embezzled from had pursued the highest amount of time incarcerated as possible. When he had been caught, the company discovered that he had been embezzling the money for over two years in the amount of over eight hundred thousand dollars. Oh my lands!!

I read article after article on this guy concluding that he was as dangerous as the reporter had wrote. When I last looked at the clock it was after two in the morning, and I knew I had to stop until later after I had some sleep. I fell into a deep sleep not waking up until almost noon the next day. After having breakfast I couldn't wait to get back on my laptop to dig more. This time I printed out most of the articles so I could read them later. The last article had even printed his picture. Not a bad looking guy, but he sure looked familiar to me. Don't know why I thought that, but there was just something about him. I then wondered if he was from the area, but I came to a dead end on that inquiry. I placed all the articles in a manila folder, and carefully tucked it in with my billing folders for work. Drew had taken two weeks off from working to be with Avery. His mom was staying for the two weeks to help with Avery, and another two weeks once Drew went back to work. I went to the main house for a visit with her often when I knew Avery was asleep for her nap. I enjoyed our visits, but thought afterwards that maybe she had planned to take a nap herself trying to keep up with Avery every day. She had insisted that she was fine. I thought it was strange that she insisted that we visit outside away from the house to chat. We sat on the little patio on the side of the garage drinking our cup of tea. That was when she asked me what I thought of Velma. Of all questions to be asked. I didn't know what to reply. I didn't want to tell her what Vivian had told me, nor the things I heard myself. I finally said she had a quirky way of saying and doing things, hoping Carolyn wouldn't ask any more questions. Carolyn felt there was something else going on with Velma that she couldn't place her finger on. Then she looked right at me telling me to keep my eyes open, and be careful, very careful.

I asked Carolyn in a nonchalantly way if she knew where Velma was originally from. Carolyn wasn't sure, but she knew it was on the paperwork the agency sent over about her when Drew and Vivian were looking for a housekeeper. Said she would find out, and let me know before she leaves to go back home. I didn't want her to think I was trying to be nosy, but I explained that sometimes if you're from another area, things we find strange are just normal to them. I thought that was a good explanation because Carolyn nodded her head as if she thought so as well. Whew, I dodged a bullet there. But I secretly hoped she would find out, and let me know!

Drew invited me to go to dinner with him, Avery, and his mom before Carolyn was heading back home. It was a very pleasant evening. When Drew went to use the restroom, Carolyn leaned over to me telling me where Velma was from. She had chummed up with Velma enough to obtain that valuable information. She also told me Velma was really angry I was still living in the little house. Vivian had told me that herself before she died stating she had heard Velma tell someone the same thing on the phone. That other person was male, and he told her she had to do something to incriminate me so I would get kicked out. Vivian had felt guilty for listening in on Velma's phone call, but she also wanted to warn me all the same. Once we saw Drew coming back we quickly changed the topic. I wasn't too concerned about getting kicked out of the house. I was pregnant with their child, it was part of the agreement for carrying and delivering their baby. Drew knew this, and he suspected it was Velma that had 'bugged' our houses, and I also felt he trusted my character. However, once we got home and he walked me to my house he asked if he could talk to me after his mother leaves. I smiled and said sure, any time. Now, that was something out of the blue, and maybe Velma did do something to get me kicked out after all. I had to stop, and think it through before I was completely paranoid over something that might not be anything at all.

# CONFESSION

---

I had seen our doctor at Vivian's funeral. He came over asking me how I was doing. I just looked at him quietly responding that I had just lost my best friend as I struggled to hold back the tears that were on the very edge of rolling down my face. He asked for me to come in the office at my earliest convenience. I had another appointment with him next Wednesday, and I will see him then. I wasn't even sure if Drew would be up to going with me to the appointment, but I surely would understood if he had declined.

Everything was fine with the baby. Once the doctor told me I was still very much connected with Vivian with the baby growing inside me. That had made a great impact on how I felt when I left his office. Drew had declined to go with me with everything going on at his office. It was too soon for me to expect him to think about anything or anyone else other than Avery, and his loss of Vivian. He was heartbroken with Vivian gone. He had other things he was dealing with that were important, even though his baby I was carrying was just as important in my opinion. But, I understood, kind of. The doctor had given me a pamphlet on grief support, in case I thought I needed it which I took, and stuffed into my purse before leaving.

After several weeks had passed I felt that the days were easier to get through. Drew had enrolled Avery at the child care center by his office, so I didn't see them as often now. I missed Avery being around with her nonstop chatter, and bouncy brown curls that Vivian had kept in little pig tails. I had decided to walk up to the house one evening when I saw they were home. Drew had just started serving up their dinner that Velma had prepared in the crock pot when I knocked. I use to just walk right in, but I decided I'd better knock this time in case he didn't want me intruding. He was pleasantly surprised to see that it was me, and asked if I would join them for dinner. We hadn't seen each other at all since the night before his mother had left to go back home, several weeks ago. Avery was so happy to see me, and chatted on and on about her new school. She never mentioned Vivian which I thought was rather odd, but she's so young, and probably thinking Vivian is just away for a few days.

After dinner while Drew got Avery ready for bed, I cleaned the kitchen for him. As I was getting ready to leave he asked he could talk to me for a little bit. He had asked me to talk with him a while back, but I was sure he had forgotten about that, and I didn't pester him about it. He wanted to talk on the patio, which I didn't think was strange that he wanted to talk there, and not in the house. Did he feel his house was bugged again? Was there a reason he didn't want me in his house? Was I being paranoid again? All these thoughts raced through my head as I waited for him to come outside, and when he did he had two tall glasses of iced tea for us. Once he handed me my glass he sat in the chair next to me, and let out a sigh of relief.

Drew apologized about talking on the patio with me. Neither one of us knew if the bugs were still in place or not. He said he tried to use the bugging device after Vivian's funeral in the house, but found it had been broken, so he was being very careful on everything being said inside, just in case there were more bugs planted. He told me a little about the case he was working on. It sounded as if it was the same case Vivian had told me about. He was very concerned of the potential danger he had placed himself, and Avery in. Vivian was right, he had been very worried, but I don't think she knew the extent of his worry. We talked for hours out there, and it seemed like Drew had just needed someone to vent to. I listened carefully to everything he had to say before I asked if he could tell me the man's name involved. When he did, I knew it was the same person the police officer had asked if I knew, and I had looked on the internet for. I told Drew I thought it was the same person. He was confused to how I knew that name, so I explained that the police officer had questioned me the day Vivian passed away, if I had knew him, or of the name.

Drew changed the topic when he thought he had said enough. I asked how Avery has been, and when he said she misses Vivian very much every day my heart sank. Poor little child I thought. He offered other information freely which I wanted to know, but didn't want to ask him yet. He had Velma coming in part-time in the mornings now. She does a little housework, and prepares meals in the crock pot for supper. He had Avery at the child care center close to his office so he could get to her if he was needed, and it also gave him a little longer time that he could be with her before he started and ended his work day. He also told me that dear Velma had asked him about living in the little house once again, which he told her he was happy with me living there for the time being. He explained to her that he had other things to worry about at the moment, and my living there wasn't one of them. Velma was miffed at his explanation, but Drew didn't care what she thought.

I think right at that moment it hit him that I was still carrying their baby. He reached over taking my hand asking how I was feeling, how the baby was doing, if I needed anything, and quickly apologized that he hasn't gone to the past few doctor appointments with me. I told him I was fine, work was going great, baby is growing, she kicks some pretty strong ones now, and I understood he had other things going on that caused him to miss the appointments. I was just happy that he took the time to talk with me that night, and finally ask me how I was doing! I didn't want to let him know I was feeling lonely being totally by myself without anyone to talk with, but he didn't need to hear that. I didn't want him to think I was whining about poor ole me after everything he has been through himself. I got up to leave telling him I needed to get home. I could walk it by myself since he had Avery in the house sleeping. He gave me a hug when I left thanking me for talking with him. I replied, "any time" and walked to my house. As I looked back at the big house once I reached my place, I saw Drew still standing on the patio waiting for me to go inside, and waved to him.

I was already in my seventh month before Drew showed up at the doctor's office. I hadn't told him to meet me there, but he was there waiting for me to arrive. He asked if he could go in with me like we had in the past. I assured him that he was welcome any time. He thought that maybe without Vivian with us that I wouldn't feel comfortable with just him being in there. I told him to stop thinking that kind of nonsense, but I did understand what he was thinking. The doctor checked me, and the baby stating we were both doing great. Ansley started kicking up a storm right then. I asked Drew if he wanted to feel her kicking. He nodded as he was placing his hand on my belly, just as she gave a hard kick. His hand was so warm on my huge belly, and immediately the baby's kicks got gentle. It was like she knew that was her daddy's hand touching her, and that she had better behave. And touching her for the first time. I noticed tears forming in Drew's eyes before he removed his hand. I could tell he was happy, and yet, sad at the same time. Drew thanked me for letting him feel Ansley's kicks, and quickly asked if I could have lunch with him after the appointment.

Over lunch he told me he was very happy to feel the baby moving, and promised he would be at the remaining doctor appointments with me. That was when I asked if he was still planning to go through with me being the surrogate. He looked as if I had slapped his face hard with that question. He said that he absolutely was going through with everything Vivian and him had agreed to from the beginning. He had no intention of changing anything. He continued looking at me, and asked what had I been thinking.

I finally admitted to him that I was concerned that since he was a single parent now that maybe one was more than enough for him, and I would be on my own with this one. By that time I had tears in my eyes waiting for his answer. He reached for my hand saying he would never do that to me, to Vivian, to Avery, and not even to himself. He has a long road ahead of him raising the girls, but knew some how or another he was going to make it. I apologized for having those thoughts rattling around in my brain, but I hadn't heard from anyone on what the plan was now. He apologized for not talking to me sooner. He has had so much on his mind that he had neglected to consider what I was feeling, or going through. I put my head down to let the tears fall freely onto my lap hoping no one saw me. Drew came over to my side of the booth to hold me in his arms where we both shed our tears together. Afterwards, we promised not to let anything like this happen again between us. We needed an open and honest policy with everything, and anything.

The weekend was almost here for the family's private 'Celebration of Life' for Vivian. Carolyn and Drew's dad, Mark, were the first to arrive a few days earlier to help with everything. They were staying in the guest room in the house, along with Drew's sister and brother's families. Vivian's family side were all local residents, so they wouldn't need any accommodations. Carolyn arranged for the food to be catered, so we wouldn't be bothering Velma with anything. Velma and Carolyn had a dislike for each other recently, and Carolyn didn't want her there while they were planning anything. Velma told Carolyn that they better pick up after themselves because she wasn't their maid. That remark had been overheard by Drew, so he gave Velma the two weeks off during the time his parents would be staying with him. Yay Drew!! It was nice that he had heard Velma's comments himself, and not just what we had told him all along.

Drew was busy with the grilling, and everyone brought dish after dish outside placing them on the tables where people would be filling their plates at. I had made a large collage of photographs of Vivian from the time she was a baby on, that Drew had. I left plenty of room for more pictures to be added by other family members, and by the time the Celebration of Life had started, it was completely full of various photos.

Everyone was having a wonderful time. Drew asked that everyone give a remembrance of something they had done with Vivian after they had finished eating. One by one the family got up to tell their memory of Vivian. Most of the things they had to say were amusing which got everyone to chuckle. Several were sad memories which brought tears to their eyes.

Drew announced that he had a letter Vivian had written over a year or so ago that he wanted me to read out loud. It was to the family, and he just couldn't read it himself without breaking down. I got up thinking it was probably a mixture of happiness, and sadness of her life with him, but it was much more than that. I took the letter from Drew as he sat down next to his parents. He whispered he was sorry to them, and nodded for me to begin. I opened it with shaky hands and began to read.

*Dear family,*

*If this is letter is being read to you, you know that I'm already gone. Please don't cry. I have had a wonderful life, the best husband I could have ever asked for, a beautiful daughter, and maybe another child or two, depending on when this letter is being read. I have a few things I want to share though, and I felt the only way I could do it was in a letter to everyone, and have it heard at the same time.*

*First, to my loving husband Drew,*

*Thank you for being the best person I could have found in my life. You have shown me love, compassion, and understanding of how to be the wife you deserved. I couldn't have done it without you. I have loved every single minute being your wife. You have always had my heart from day one. Whenever I felt I was sinking in quicksand, you were there to pull me out. You were my rock helping me make sense of things I didn't understand, and you were the best person cheering me on when I had felt I couldn't do things. You were my everything!*

*I will love you forever Drew.*


*To my Mom and Dad,*

*Thank you for being my parents, for raising me with great morals and values, being supportive of my decisions, and helping me become the person I grew to be. I couldn't have done it without you.*


*Drew's parents,*

*Thank you for having Drew! He has been my everything. The two of you did a great job raising a gentle, and kind man. I loved him from the moment we met. You accepted me into your family without any misgivings, and I always treasured our times with you.*

*Dear Allison,*

*Thank you for being my very first best friend from the time we met. I could always count on you to listen, and understand my feelings. You have blessed me in more ways than you could ever know, and I will never forget that. Always remember that you are family forever.*

*Now with those few that I have wrote to at this time, I also must tell you I have been deceitful at the same time. I am not sorry for it either. Not one time have I ever keep anything from any of you, but this time it is a biggie. You all know how much I always wanted to be a mother. That was always my dream, and after having all the miscarriages, which broke my heart, I didn't give up. You see, I was always able to get pregnant, it was my body that would reject the baby later. I was always left heart broken. Don't think I didn't hear the many comments from some of you when we announced Avery's pregnancy to everyone. I heard too many nasty comments to think about. I want you to know those comments were very rude, and extremely hurtful to me. I needed my family to be happy for me, and to wish us the best, not to question Drew and my decisions, or think I was just selfish to put myself though another pregnancy that would end up the same way as the others had. We didn't want to adopt someone's baby, we wanted our baby. And we finally got OUR baby with Avery. I was over the moon when she was born, and couldn't have been happier.*

*You are probably wondering what does this have to do with deceit. It has everything to do with the information we've kept from everyone. I'm sorry you are learning about this in a letter, but even after Avery was born, there were other comments made, but this time they were directed at my best friend, Ali. I was shocked and hurt for the things I heard my family say about you Ali. I am so sorry for those things. Before Avery was born, and Ali was also pregnant, you had made mean and nasty comments about her giving her baby up when it was born. Why didn't Drew and I just adopt Ali's baby since she she wasn't keeping it herself? Hang on family….. the reason we couldn't "**adopt**" Ali's baby was because the baby in her belly, was our baby, Avery.*

*Ali was so gracious to become a surrogate for us. Ali unselfishly gave up her time, effort, and womb to help us have a baby we had desperately wanted. I wore a fake belly to keep my pregnancy going, and kept quiet. Didn't you ever think it was rather odd that I never let any of you feel my baby moving? Well, now you know why.*

*Drew and I decided we wanted another baby, and we approached Ali to see if she was willing to do it again, and she was willing to help us once again. So, whether I have Avery and no other child, well, that will be seen at a later date. But, if there's another baby in our family, my hope is that you all will be happy for us. And, not judge us like you had*

113

*in the past.*

*I am asking that you understand why we felt we had to do it this way, and to please keep this information you have just received quiet for more than one reason or another. Are we ashamed of what we have done? That is not a question that needs to be asked by anyone, because we are **not**. **Not one single bit**. If you think we should be, then you need to get over it and yourself.*

*I love you all, and hope the family can understand why we did it this way. I hope you all can respect our decisions even if you don't agree with them. Just be kind to one another.*

*Love you always,*

*Vivian*

I finished reading the letter through tears in my eyes, and saw tears in just about everyone's eyes as well. No one spoke for several minutes. I hoped they were digesting the information they had just received. It was Vivian's mom who came up to me to thank me for helping her daughter become the mother she had always wanted to be. She gave me a hug, and told me it had made her daughter extremely happy to be a mother.

Drew asked if he could talk to his parents, and Vivian's parents privately, away from the rest of the siblings. He quickly added for me to be there as well. We went to the side of the garage to be far enough away, where Drew was sure he wouldn't be heard. He said he was not there to apologize to anyone, but he wanted to tell them that there was more news. Carolyn was the first one who immediately said there was no need for him to think he had to apologize to anyone. What and how they did things was from their heart. Drew and Vivian owed no one an apology. What they had done, and why they had done it the way they did, was nobodies business, but their own. He thanked her, and said he hoped everyone would understand why they had it done that way. I paused for a few minutes, lost in thought on how he was going to tell them the next piece of news. I knew what he was going to tell them without him telling me in advance. His head was bowed down, and his hands clasped in front of his face with his index fingers touching his trembling lips. No one spoke a word or moved an inch until he was ready to talk. He took in a deep breath lifting his head up, and pulled me next to him before saying anything more. I could see the puzzlement in everyone's eyes. When Drew took in a gulp of air he nodded his head, and told them that Vivian and him were expecting another baby in about two months. I could tell they hadn't expected to receive news like that, and they were in shock. Complete shock! Drew told them Vivian knew before she had passed away that they were having another girl, thanks to Allison here. No one moved until Mark shook Drew's hand congratulating him. Both Mark and Carolyn hugged me before Vivian's parents ever moved an inch. Finally, they smiled saying they couldn't be any more happier than when they held Avery for the first time. I let out a sigh of relief.

The five of us walked back to the others who had been busy chatting while we were gone. Drew was about to tell the others what was said with the parents when his sister, Susan, had asked if by chance, was I pregnant for him and Vivian now? I let Drew answer that question, and I could see everyone, except Vivian's sisters, were truly happy for Drew.

Once everyone was over the shock of the news and congratulations, Drew also told them about another piece of news. He told them they couldn't talk about any of this information in the house, because both our houses had been bugged, and he didn't trust Velma the housekeeper, knowing anything of this. He also told everyone he was working on a case that had involved Joshua Jones from some years ago. Joshua was a very dangerous man, and was ready to be released on parole in about seven more months. Joshua had made it very clear that he would get even with Drew for losing his first case, which caused him to go to prison. So, he was asking everyone for their help for the next few months, and especially after the baby was born. I watched as everyone nodded their heads. Carolyn spoke first saying they'd be more than happy to help. I heard more family say they'd pitch in, too. That was great knowing they would be there to help Drew through everything.

That's what family is about. I'm sure Vivian was watching down from heaven smiling that the family would be there to help with anything that he needed.

# DISCOVERY

<hr>

Drew had talked with me the other day saying he didn't think I should walk along the fence line by myself anymore. Things on this case he was working on wasn't an easy task, and he had concerns about something dreadful happening to all of us down the road. I told him I had a treadmill in the basement that I'll use instead, which had pleased him.

Drew continued to grill steaks on Saturdays through the rest of the summer, and into the early fall for everyone. That seemed to be the only time we had the chance to talk freely. Even then he wasn't sure what was safe to say to anyone anymore. I told him I stayed away from the house when he isn't there because I didn't care for Velma. He told me things were being moved in his office, or files come up missing one day, and back in the desk again the next day. I told him maybe he needs to install cameras like nanny cams to find out who was snooping, and why. He hadn't thought about the nanny cams, and decided he was going to look into getting them. I was sure Vivian would have told him the same thing if she had been here.

He had Officer Pete get him another bugging device to use. We both thought the other one had been broken on purpose, and probably by Velma herself. A few things had been said in the house over the phone that Velma had asked Drew about later. Drew felt there was only one way Velma could have had that information. I told him there were many times Velma would comment to Vivian about watching a certain movie, and it happened to be a movie that they had recently watched. That had happened more than a dozen times. It gave Vivian the creeps that she was either being spied on some how, or listened to.

Officer Pete brought another bug detector over the following day, and we went through both houses finding over two dozen bugging devices strategically placed once again. I can't believe my house had several again as well. I'm home most of the time, so whomever placed them had to have seen me leave so they could get inside without being noticed. All different locations than in the past.

Officer Pete said Drew needed to put motion lights outside with sensors, so he can watch any activity on his computer of the backyard, and the rooms in the house. He recommended a company that can install them on Saturdays when Velma wouldn't be working. They could be placed in areas where they wouldn't stick out. Drew was grateful for all the information, and decided he'd call, but not until he was in his downtown office. He didn't trust that all the bugs were found once again in the houses.

The following weekend Drew had his motion sensor lights installed. Every area around the house could be seen on the computer with, or without the motion lights, and using the nanny cams on the inside. I couldn't tell where they had installed the nanny cams inside until Drew had shown me. I don't think Velma will be able to spot them either. That company had done an amazing job!

I was seeing the doctor every two weeks now, and everything was still going great. Drew seemed more involved with the appointments saying he looked forward to them. I think that was because he could feel the baby moving in my belly, and it was being done in a medical clinic. He had the warmest hands every time he gently placed them on my belly. It was as if he was afraid if he pushed too hard it would hurt little Ansley. Drew and I would have lunch together at a nearby cafe before he had to get back to the office, and I went home after each doctor visit. Drew shared information about the case a little more each time we had lunch. I could tell he was working hard on it from the different things he had said.

When I got home I looked for the file I had made on Joshua, but my entire file was gone. Everything I pulled up on the internet, and printed off was gone. I distinctly remember putting that file with my other file folders from work, so I could look at them later. Made me wonder when they could have disappeared. I hadn't thought anymore about them since I printed them that night. I immediately texted Drew on my cell phone asking if I could talk to him later that night.

He invited me up for dinner, and after getting Avery to bed we sat outside on the patio. He was still determined not to talk about anything inside the house. I told him I had a file folder full of articles on Joshua Jones that I had placed with my work folders, that was now missing. I couldn't tell him when they were taken because I hadn't looked at them since that night I printed them off the computer. Drew's eyes were wide, and I could tell he was angry from the grit his jaw took on.

I quickly told him it was probably wrong of me to look at the information on Joshua Jones, and I quickly apologized for doing that. He wasn't concerned about me doing that, just concerned that they had been taken. And who was the person who had taken them. And when did they have the time to take them considering I'm home most of the time. He said anything on the Internet was free game. He also told me he'd bring me other articles he had in his downtown office to read if I wanted them. I thought I would like to see what Drew was up against, so I nodded my head yes.

Drew had everything set up for the baby in the nursery the following weekend. The plan was that when I deliver Ansley, his mother was going to come up for a month to help. He would give Velma two weeks off paid, to keep her away from the house. When it was time for Velma to start back to work his sister would be there for a few days passing Ansley off as hers, and that he would be helping her out as long as he needed to. Velma will surely wonder where my baby was so Drew asked me to be pregnant a little longer as we had before with Avery, by wearing Vivian's fake bellies. It sounded plausible, and hoped it worked.

It wasn't more than two weeks later that I started having labor pains. I was glad Velma had already left the house to go home for the weekend when they started. I texted Drew at his office asking him to leave early to please come home because I was in labor. Then I texted Vivian's mom to tell her, because she was needed at the house to watch Avery. The pains started getting longer and harder before anyone ever made it to the house. Vivian's parents were the first to arrive, and came to see me at my house. I was in so much pain by then. Drew drove right back to my house to get me in his car, and he handed Avery over to Vivian's mom. Her parents hugged me wishing me well as I got into the car.

Drew wasted no time getting me to the hospital. It was ten miles away, and the traffic was already heavy. He put his emergency flashers on, and honking the car horn all the way there. I no sooner got undressed, and on the bed that my water had broke. The doctor was just finishing up delivering another baby, and then would be with me. But, this baby wasn't waiting, and nothing was going to stop her from coming out.

Drew had his gown already on, with the help of a

nurse, and was by my side before the doctor made it in. The natal nurse checked me telling me not to push until someone was there to catch the baby. I couldn't stop it, and before I knew it, Drew stepped over just in time to catch Ansley as she came out. I had never expected him to do that, but I was so glad he had. Ansley let out a cry just as the doctor opened the delivery room door to come in. He looked at Drew holding Ansley in his arms, and smiled thanking him for being quick on his feet. Drew held Ansley as the nurse prepped everything for Drew to cut the umbilical cord. The doctor watched as Drew was handed the shears to cut the cord while holding his daughter. The happiness radiated off his face as he held her close to his chest with tears flowing down his face.

Shortly he walked over to me handing me his daughter to hold. He bent over whispering that Vivian would be as happy as he was right then, before kissing my cheek. Ansley was a perfect baby with a mass of dark hair, and a great complexion for being a newborn. Ansley had every feature as Vivian. No wonder why Drew broke down into tears. I knew Vivian was watching from above, and pleased that she had another girl.

I handed Ansley back to Drew while the doctor finished working on me. Drew went with the nurse as she cleaned, measured, and weighed Ansley. She was so close to being the same size as Avery was at birth, just two ounces more.

Once everything was done I was taken to my room, Drew came in rolling the baby's little newborn size crib in front of him wearing a huge smile on his face. He stopped next to my bed giving me a hug, and another kiss on the cheek before asking if it was okay with me that he stays with us. I didn't have a problem with that. At least we didn't have to go through what we had to the last time I delivered.

I heard Ansley start to cry later in the night, and woke up just as Drew had picked her up from the crib to feed her. He was pretty good trying not to wake me, but I was awake. I sat up watching him, and after he finished getting a burp from Ansley, and putting on a dry diaper, he placed her back down for a few more hours sleep.

I told him he was a pro at being a daddy to a newborn again. He said he was trying not to wake me, and apologized that he didn't succeed in doing that. There was no need to apologize. I didn't mind it one bit. It gave me another chance to see her beautiful face. I laid back down, and was back to sleep in matter of a few minutes.

The next day we had several visitors. I asked to be wheeled out to the sun room so I could give Drew, and the family time alone. They needed to bond with the new baby, and especially with Vivian not being there to celebrate with them, I'm sure was it was difficult for everyone, too.

Carolyn came to the sun room giving me a big hug. She knew why I wasn't in the room while the family was there, and told me they were so happy Vivian and I had become best of friends, and that I had done this for them again. I told her Vivian knew I was carrying a baby girl, and even got to feel the baby move in my belly before she passed away. That was when I started to tear up. Vivian was gone, and will never get the chance to watch her babies grow up. She had been short changed, but I was going to make sure both girls would always know what a wonderful mommy they had. We both starting crying then.

Drew walked in the sun room as we were crying, and came over putting his arms around both of us. He knew why we were upset without having to ask. It had been more emotional than what I had thought I would be this time. Avery was being walked down the hall with her other grandmother until she saw me. She dropped her grandmother's hand, and ran to me. She said she had a baby sister, and she loved her. She wanted to know if I saw her yet. I nodded I had, and that she was just as precious as she was herself. I was glad she couldn't put two and two together on everything that had happened. Avery wanted me to come see her new baby sister, and was trying to push the wheelchair towards the room. Drew stepped in to help her push me.

Visiting hours were over, and everyone had to leave, except Drew. Everyone hugged me as they left, and I settled back into the bed. I was glad when they brought me my dinner because I was starving. I missed my lunch, but saw little bites had been taken out of the sandwich I had ordered for lunch, and knew Avery was hungry herself. I didn't mind, but I was ready to chow down my dinner as soon as it was placed on my table. They had brought one for Drew as well, and what he didn't eat, I ate that, too!

Going home was going to be hard. Drew would be

driving me home with Ansley while the family members were waiting at the house. I asked him to drop me off first at my house so I could go to bed to sleep. I didn't feel sleepy at all, but I didn't want to be at the house with everyone else there. This was their time to be with Drew, and his girls. I would have time after they leave to be with the girls whenever I wanted. I knew Carolyn wouldn't mind me coming up to the house to visit.

I was concerned about Velma minding though, for some reason. And the first day I went up to visit Carolyn wearing my fake belly it was all I could do to not slap Velma in the face. She was complaining about the extra work it was causing her that day. She said Drew's sister had a baby, and just knew she was going to pawn it off to Drew somehow. She just knew that was going to happen, and when it does, she was going to leave. Drew still had Velma coming in part-time, just for the mornings. Velma was very pleased with that arrangement, and remarked that maybe his sister would wash the extra clothes herself. Then she told me how glad she was that I wasn't going to keep my baby. She certainly wasn't going to put up with a house full of crying babies all the time. That was the only thing that I could chuckle about….she'll never know anything different.

Once the doctor cleared me from having the baby I had planned to do a good heavy cleaning in my house. I had been slacking on the cleaning the last few weeks of my pregnancy, and it showed. It didn't take me long to clean it though. I decided to tackle the basement the next day. I wanted to get back on the treadmill, and maybe add a stationary bicycle to my workout.

After I had swept the entire basement floor, I rinsed it off with the garden hose aiming the water towards the drain. I opened the windows to help it dry faster before putting down the area rug I used under my treadmill. I thought I'd organize the room allowing me more space by putting the equipment closer to the stairs. That was when I felt a breeze coming from the wall. I thought that was rather strange to have a breeze coming from that area. I ran upstairs to get my little flashlight to see where it was coming from.

The only thing along that wall were shelves. Some for storage tubs, and one was for empty canning jars. The jars have been there for some time from the dust that had collected on their lids. I never removed the canning jars because for one thing, they weren't mine, and the other thing was that I hadn't planned on living here that long to bother throwing them away.

I turned on my flashlight scanning the entire shelf unit. It was definitely coming somewhere from behind the canning jars. I had a small piece of paper that I tied to a string to see if it was just circulation from the open windows, but it was clear as day that it was coming from behind the shelf of the jars. I took an old metal coat hanger running it along the top of the shelf, and I was able to push it way back into the wall. The garage was on that side, so I ran upstairs to see if I could see the coat hanger come through on the garage floor, but the coat hanger wasn't sticking out any where.

I ran back downstairs to check if the coat hanger had

slipped out of place, but it was still shoved through the wall where I had put it. I was baffled. I felt around the entire section, and was able to feel the breeze all along it. I pulled the coat hanger out, and pulled on the shelf. It didn't move one iota. So, I thought I would push it, and it moved backwards into the wall. I was stunned. I continued to push harder until it wouldn't budge anymore. I took my flashlight peering inside the dark damp area. All I could see at the time was nothing but huge spiderwebs. Lots and lots of old clinging spiderwebs hanging from the ceiling, and walls. I needed a better, and brighter flashlight to look anymore.

Once Velma had left for the day I went to Drew's garage to locate a high beam flashlight. I was determined to find out why there was this hidden space under my garage. I figured it was probably just a root cellar that was used in the olden days. I rushed back to my house, and down the stairs to my new found discovery. I flicked on the flashlight switch, and cautiously peered around the corner of the shelf preparing for a bat, or something to come flying out at me. Nothing came out which I was very glad about.

I found a switch, like an old light switch on the wall. I flipped it on thinking nothing would happen, but I was wrong. Lights came on behind the shelf unit illuminating a rather small room. I grabbed my broom I had been sweeping the floor with, before I ventured past the shelf to sweep away the spiderwebs before entering any farther.

I could see everything much better once my eyes

adjusted to the dimly lit room. I could now see that there were light bulbs illuminating a long hallway, or possible tunnel. What the heck could this be? I wondered if it was smart of me to see where it led to, or just get out as soon as possible before something terrible could go wrong. I wanted to know, and decided I would check it out. It seemed as if I had walked miles before I came to the end. All there was in front of me was a wooden wall. Nothing suggesting that I could go further if I had wanted to, just a plain wooden wall in front of me.

I knew I had better get out of there as soon as I could, but not before I noticed another light switch on the wall just like the one on my end. I reached for it, not thinking that it would do anything. I hesitated before I turned the switch thinking maybe I would be swallowed into a hole in the floor, like a hidden trap, or something set to keep people out. I felt along the door, and I could feel air escaping out to where-ever it was going. Without thinking another thought I turned that switch, and the lights went out in the tunnel. I quickly turned it again which turned the lights back on.

I decided I would come back after Velma leaves tomorrow to check it out more. Until then, I would finish cleaning my basement by placing my treadmill in another corner of the basement. I turned to leave, and decided to count my paces to see how far I had walked underground. I would go outside, and pace the yard to see where it stopped. Since the tunnel was straight I felt it would be an easy task.

I turned the lights off on my end of the tunnel, and

carefully slid the canning jar shelf back in to its position that I had found it in. There were hooped ropes hanging on each side of the shelf that I pulled towards me, which put the shelf right back into place. Someone had gone to a lot of trouble to erect this tunnel, and disguise it from being found out easily. There weren't any scrapping marks on the floor like I had expected from opening the hidden door. Smart people had to have done this for some reason, and I was planning to find out why.

When I had re-entered my garage, I counted out my paces before going outside to continue toward the house. I stopped just before the house about two paces too short. I felt it was still feasible that it led right to the house thinking that I may have paced one or two steps shorter than I did under ground, but none the less, I knew where it must have come to. The house. Now to find out why!

# THREATS AND SAFETY

All through the night I thought about that tunnel wondering why it was there before it had dawned me. Many of these older homes in this area were part of the Underground Railroad. I wondered if this tunnel could have been one of them. That made perfect sense to me. The big house was built during that time period, and Lake Erie wasn't many more miles north of the property. I decided tomorrow I would go to the library after I was finished with my work to see if there were any homes listed as part of the Underground Railroad in our neighborhood. I may have stumbled on something historic, and I bet Drew has no idea about the tunnel.

I flew through my work anticipating of finding out some information on the house, and if it was part of the Underground Railroad. The librarian was very helpful, and very insightful on the history of the houses involved with the Underground Railroad in the area. I was impressed with everything she knew, and what she had shared with me. There was so much to learn about this area that I found to be interesting.

However, we came to a quick halt because I didn't know the first owners names that owned the property. So, we tried with the address. Still no news, and that could be because the street and road names had been changed at one time. Road names weren't recorded because they were county, and very few people lived on them back then. She offered to research it for me some more, and would give me a call when, and if she found any information pertaining to our house. I couldn't tell her I had found a tunnel under the yard, so I told her I was just interested in the area knowing many homes were part of the historic event. I wasn't raised there, but found the area to be very interesting. That was enough to satisfy her.

As I was about to pull in the driveway, the gate was already opening up. Velma sneered at me when she passed by my car on her way out. I gave her a kind smile back while other thoughts were running through my mind of what I actually wanted to do. I was glad she was gone so I could see if there was anything new in the tunnel.

I hurried to my house flying down the basement stairs as fast as I could. I would be able check the wall at the end of the tunnel without worrying of being heard. I moved my wall, flicked on the light switch, and was on my way with the flashlight in my hand. I wasn't nearly as scared as I had been yesterday when I had no idea what to expect when I made my maiden run through it. I was at the other dead end wall in a matter of a few minutes. This time I noticed there was a wooden slot on each side of the ending wall. I carefully took them off, and grabbed the looped ropes next to them giving them a tug.

The wall moved out just like the one on my end. I wasn't as surprised as I thought I would be when it was finally opened completely. I walked through the opening right into Drew's basement. I looked back at the space I had just emerged from, and it too, was a shelf full of empty canning jars from top to bottom. I was really intrigued at the thought that it was a well hidden secret apparently from everyone. Everyone, but me!

I closed everything back up, and went back to my end of the tunnel. I noticed the backside of my wall also had the wooden slots, and ropes in the same places. I figured the wooden slots were used as a way to lock the door from the inside. Safety measures I suppose. Safety from what, I wondered.

Saturday couldn't get here fast enough so I could share what I had discovered with Drew. I told him I had a big surprise for him when he had the extra time. It happened to be the weekend that Vivian's parents took the girls, too. They started taking Avery when she was little every third weekend, and as soon as Ansley was old enough, she went there, too. Gave them grandparents time with the girls.

Drew called me saying he was up, and was wondering

what this big surprise was that I had wanted to tell him about. I told him to go on the patio, and don't take his eyes off my house. Not for a second. He chuckled, but did what I had asked him to do. I waved at him from my front door before scrambling down to the tunnel. I was at his house quickly pulling the wall open. I went up the stairs to the kitchen, and out the opened back door. Drew was standing there still watching my house when I asked him if he'd like some iced tea. He swung around with the most puzzled look on his face. He scratched his head asking how I did that?

I motioned for him to follow me, and he did. I gave him the 'sshh' indication using my fingers to my lips to not say anything in the kitchen, or basement. I didn't trust the area to be bug free. When I showed him the shelf unit, which I had kept open, his mouth dropped. I motioned for him to enter it with me handing him his flashlight as I pulled the wall shut behind us. After we were in the tunnel I told him I had discovered it the other day when I was rearranging my treadmill in my basement, and had felt a slight breeze coming from the canning jars shelf.

I somehow had gained enough nerve to investigate it. He was shocked that there was a tunnel like that connecting his house to mine. When we were in the little room at my end of the tunnel he was in disbelief. I pulled the door shut, and showed him there weren't any marks left on the basement floor to indicate that there had been something opened there. He was at a loss for words. I told him that it may have been part of the Underground

Railroad to help the slaves escape to Canada at one time. He just shook his head in bewilderment. The tunnel had been well constructed, and stood the time of not being used lately.

After I shut everything up, we went outside away from the house before we talked again. Maybe there was another reason for the tunnel being there, but I felt it was used as part of the Underground Railroad, but more than likely it was for another purpose. Maybe used as a tornado shelter, who knows. I went on telling him that I had gone to the library to see if I could find any information on it, or the area, but found nothing directly connected to his house. I hadn't spoke a word of it to anyone except him. He admitted that he was glad of that. He chuckled saying, if anything, we should set a few chairs down there, and talk freely, because he was certain Velma didn't know anything about it either. She surely would have said something to Vivian if she had known.

Drew was right, we could talk freely in there, and no one would be able to hear us. In fact, I checked the other day, and there wasn't phone service in it either. Only up against the door did I get a signal, and it was a very low signal at that. We both wondered why there was a room at my end of the tunnel, and not his. We were going to check into it more, but until then, mum was the word.

Drew asked if I liked to play tennis to change the subject. Apparently, he was headed out to the clubhouse when he remembered I had wanted to see him. Told him I loved playing tennis, but I didn't feel like I was very good at it. He asked me to join him at the club, and we could hit a few balls, and see if I wanted to engage in a game against him. I was stoked that I had been asked. I played tennis in college on a team, but hadn't played since. I had a great time, and I actually won a match against Drew. Yes, I still had it as I punched the air with my fist!!

We went to the clubhouse for lunch where Drew gave me my own membership card to the place. I could come, and go whenever I wanted now. I could practice to regain lost skills at being better when, and if, we play again. I thought I better get the stationary bike soon so I could strengthen my legs more because they were sure throbbing now.

When we got back to the house we sat on the patio next to each other talking quietly about that case he was working on. It was getting close to the time for it to be back in the court room. Drew wasn't happy about them planning to release Joshua Jones at all. I told him the town Joshua Jones had grown up in, which he didn't have any information on that on any papers for some reason. It was just as if he had plopped out of the sky. Guess Joshua was good at embezzling money because he had a string of other people, and companies he had done it to in his past. Drew admitted that he didn't regret losing the case, and causing Joshua to go to prison, because what he had done was wrong. Drew had worked hard on the case, but the other side had more information to produce than what Drew had, and the jury members were the ones that decided that he was guilty.

Early the next morning Drew was knocking on my

door. I was still asleep, but got up quickly to answer. I barely had my robe on when I let him in the house. He asked if he could talk to me as he pointed down towards the basement. I knew what he was referring to, the tunnel. I quickly dressed into shorts, and tank top, and followed him. As we were going through the garage, I grabbed the two folding lawn chairs hanging on the wall taking them with us. No sense in having to stand the entire time in the tunnel room.

Once we closed the door behind us to what we now referred to as 'the cave', Drew opened the chairs for us to sit on. He had thought through the night about the tunnel. Then the court case. Then it hit him that if things got too irrational on the case, to where he felt there might be some danger to the girls, the cave would be the perfect place to hide them in, if necessary. I told him it was an excellent place, and that maybe we should get it ready in case it did come down to that.

Right then, the lights flickered, and went completely out. I froze in my chair barely breathing. We didn't think about bringing a flashlight with us either. I can tell you, it was pitch black inside that little room. I barely got out a whisper asking Drew if he was still in his lawn chair when the lights came back on. I knew no one was at the other end because I had secured it when we came through it last, so it couldn't be opened from the other side. And, we closed this side when we were in the cave. Drew got up to look at the wiring, finding that it was extremely old, and not safe to be using. We sat back down to get our wits back when Drew decided he would need to replace the wiring as soon as possible. Now wasn't soon enough, and asked if I'd like to go to the hardware store with him to get a few things. I was more than ready to get out of the tunnel before the lights went out again.

As soon as we got out of the tunnel, and closed the door, I grabbed a tablet of paper from upstairs, and we were heading to the store. Drew rattled off several items he would need for me to write down on the paper as he drove. I thought maybe we should get a few other items to place down there as well. If we would have to be down there with the girls for any length of time, they would need a few things to occupy themselves, and something for them to sleep on. I thought of other things as well, as we shopped that I jotted down to go over with Drew when he was done gathering the electrical supplies he needed. I had never known of a man to take longer than a woman at shopping than what Drew was taking that day in the hardware store!

We needed to be back at the house in three hours, so the girls could be dropped off from their weekend at Vivian's parents. Drew was serious about using the cave as a safe area, and wanted to make it as comfortable as possible if we ever had to use it. It was going to take time getting the electrical work completed without anyone knowing. He would have to wait until the girls were in bed asleep for the night before he dared to start the project. Avery would remember too much, and possibly blurt it out to Velma, which would defeat the purpose of having it as a safe place.

I offered to take the wiring through the tunnel on my side, and string it along the sides in the afternoon, after Velma left to go home. Drew thought that would be a great help. Drew said he would drop the girls off at child care, and come back in the afternoon to get it started. I offered to watch the kids at night if he needed more time. We'd have to get a long extension cord to provide the light while he worked on it. Plans were coming in rapid session on getting this done as quickly as possible. I wrote the timeline out on my tablet of paper, and stuffed it into my purse.

Drew got started on the wiring right away. He made it to the house right after Velma had left for the day to get it started, and I would pick the girls up at the child care for him in the evening. Drew had put my name down as an emergency person, as well as the girl's grandparents, so any of us could pick them up if necessary. The girls were always happy to see me. I think I was just as happy as them because they mean so much to me.

Drew had the wiring done by the end of the week, and I put the various items I purchased in the room. A blow up mattress, a cooler, battery operated lanterns, extra batteries for the flashlights and lanterns, heavy blankets, and things for the girls to play with. I thought I had everything needed, but thought that night lying in bed of a few more items like a first aid kit, snacks, extra diapers, powder, wipes, and a potty chair for Avery. We left the folding chairs there as Drew and I would go down there to talk when we needed to in private. He was happy I had thought of the other items, and hoped the time never came to have to use them. But it was better to be prepared than not.

A few times during the week I would sneak through the tunnel, and listen at the kitchen door to what Velma was talking about when she was on the phone. She was always talking to her brother Buddy, on plans to do something. Something big was being planned, and it would make them some big bucks was all I could gather from the conversation. Velma would never say what the plans were, or how they would get the big bucks, but it sounded like it was an evil plan to me! Whatever it was, it was going to happen soon, and she'd chuckle a sinister laugh saying it was going to be so cool to finally get even. They had waited all these years, and the pay back was going to be great. He would deserve every bit of it. Every bit of what? Hmmm, I wondered. I had heard enough, and decided to get away from the door before getting caught. That would be embarrassing, and hard to explain what I was doing there.

Drew asked me out to dinner that night when he came home. Whatever Velma had made didn't smell good to him, and I think he was getting tired of the same thing that she cooked every week. Avery wanted macaroni and cheese, and whatever she ate, Ansley would eat, too. Both girls loved to go out to eat, and they were so well behaved at their young age. It was always a pleasure to eat out with them. We went to a nice restaurant that had a kids menu that Avery looked over as if she could read, and always decided on the macaroni and cheese regardless. I knew that would be her choice. While we waited for the food to be served, Avery colored her placemat with the crayons the server provided.

Drew handed me a piece of paper folded up. I opened it, and was shocked what it had said. It was a handwritten threat made to Drew, and his two girls. It was on his desk at his downtown office when he arrived that morning. No one saw anyone strange in his office that worked there, but that note was there when Drew arrived. He looked at me whispering that we needed to be very diligent of our surroundings from now on. I asked if it was the first letter he had received like that. He shook his head no. My lands, what was going on? He said we'll talk later when the girls are asleep.

I quickly gave them their bath that night, and had them ready for bed. Avery was in a single bed now, and Ansley was only nine months old still sleeping in a crib yet. Drew had them in the same room, which he explained that if he had to hurry to them he could, for whatever reason. After reading that letter, I understood his reasoning completely.

Drew came upstairs to give the girls their good-night kiss as he tucked them in their beds. We went out to the patio where Drew told me he has been watching the security nanny cams daily. Velma, and this guy has been searching for something in his office on a daily basis lately. I told him it must be her brother Buddy. Why would they snoop in his office the way they were? What were they looking for? It didn't make any sense. Nothing she was doing had made any sense lately. I told Drew I had been listening in on Velma's conversations with her brother at the kitchen door a few times. She was definitely up to something, but I could never figure out what it could be. Drew was saving all the footage on his computer from the nanny cams just in case it led to something sinister.

I sure didn't have an easy time falling asleep that night. I tossed and turned most of the night thinking about that letter Drew had shown me. I could only imagine what Drew had been going through. He didn't have just himself to worry about, but he had two daughters to worry about as well. He had much more to deal with than what I had.

The next morning I could tell he hadn't slept well. His parents were coming for a day visit on their way home from his sister's place. I told him to get more sleep, and I would care for the girls. He was glad I offered that, and took me up on it immediately. I took them to my house, so it would stay quiet for him to sleep.

I had bought several children's books on exploring different places at the book store the other day. I had picked out one that was about exploring dark caves, and how much fun it could be. Avery was having me read it to them several times daily. I thought it would be good to introduce her to something like that, in case we did have to go to "the cave". I didn't want her to be so scared that she'd scream, and our secret of our where-a-bouts would be known. We colored caves of what she thought they would be like after reading the story. I told her I knew where there was a cave, and I might be able to take her to one sometime down the road. That excited her more than what I had expected. I found several packages of glow in the dark animals like colorful frogs, butterflies, and lady bugs at the book store that I thought I would glue them on the walls in the cave, and stars to put on the ceiling. Anything to make it kid friendly, and not so scary.

I heard Carolyn and Mark pull in the drive way so I gathered Ansley into my arms, and with Avery at my side, we met them in the driveway. Drew must have heard them as well, because he came out to greet them. They couldn't stay long, but long enough for a nice steak on the grill. Mark smiled as he handed Drew the package of steaks they had brought with them, and the grill was heating up in no time. I had plenty of left over macaroni salad to add, and opened a large can of ranch beans to heat on the grill. We didn't need much more. Everything was delicious, and we were stuffed. I enjoy their visits every time. Carolyn held Ansley most of the time while Avery showed her all the pictures she drew of a cave. Carolyn was impressed with her drawings, and I explained I had read a book to the girls about caves. That made logical sense to me, and Carolyn didn't make anything more about it.

It wasn't more than a week later I heard Drew leave earlier than usual for work. I looked out the window, and he was in a hurry. He didn't have the girls with him to take to the day care center either. I quickly got dressed so I could get the girls out of Velma's care. She had made it a well-known fact that she didn't like kids at all. Buddy was already there for some reason, and why I took a picture of his license plate on his van when I walked passed, I don't know, but I did.

As I was about to open the back door I heard Velma yell at the girls to eat, and Buddy asking Velma how long it would take for the girls to be asleep. Velma wasn't sure, but said it would be long enough for the two of them to get the papers they needed from the safe, and be on the road with the girls with them. Things weren't making any sense to me. I listened a few more minutes before Velma and Buddy had headed for the stairs to Drew's office. I couldn't go through the door to get the girls because there was a noise that would alert the people inside the house that a door had been opened. I would have been heard coming in, so I decided to run back to my house, and go through the tunnel.

I ran through the tunnel quickly, and up the basement stairs to the kitchen door. It didn't sound like anyone was in the kitchen, so I quickly and quietly opened the door. Ansley was slumped over fast asleep in her high chair, and Avery was pretty groggy sitting in her booster chair. She didn't make a sound when she saw me as I opened the door further. I knew she was pretty much drugged by then.

I scooped Ansley out of her high chair, and took Avery's hand to follow me. I whispered to her to be very quiet, and that we were going to go find a cave. She didn't show any excitement on her face, or make any noise when I told her that, as I led her to the basement door and down the stairs.

Soon, we were inside the tunnel, and I pulled the door shut behind us. I locked it on my side. Avery was having a hard time staying awake by the minute, and was having a difficult time standing up. I had Ansley in my arms, and ended up carrying Avery on my hip as we made it through the long tunnel. It slowed us down from getting to the other end, but once we got there I laid them on the blow up mattress covering them with the blankets.

I rushed upstairs to my kitchen to get the box of snacks I had put together, and a gallon of milk for the girls to drink. My phone rang startling me. It was Drew, and he was out of breath as he told me to get the girls, and get in the tunnel immediately. We were in danger. He had already notified the police, and they were on their way. I told him I already had them in the tunnel, they had been drugged, and would need an ambulance called for them as well. I didn't know what Velma had given them, but they were out cold.

Drew was on his way, and would be there within minutes. As I was closing the door of the tunnel I heard the sirens in the distance. Then I heard Velma yelling for me. She was really angry. I slid that tunnel door closed as fast as I could, and latched it. Grabbing the flashlight I turned the tunnel lights out, and laid down with the girls on the mattress. There wasn't any light around us, and it started to get very creepy.

I was sure I had heard gun shots several minutes later. I froze hoping it was just something banging around somewhere. I knew we were safe, but how safe I wasn't sure. I heard several more gun shots, and they sounded like they were right outside my house. Was my imagination getting the better of me? I checked the girls to be sure they were still covered, and scooted closer to them so I could put my arm around both of them.

These poor girls and Drew had been through more than enough in their life time. First with losing their mother, and now this. Ansley was too small to remember what had happened over the months, but Avery was old enough to where she was asking questions every now and then.

I prayed that we would be safe in the tunnel room, and Drew would come for us soon. But, time was dragging on, and when I checked the time on my phone under the blankets, so there wouldn't be any light noticed, three hours had passed already. Drew should have been there by now to get us. I was getting worried something dreadful had happened to him. I knew he would come for us if he could, but why wasn't he? Another few hours passed, and still no Drew. Could something have happened to Drew? To the police? Was there a standoff between Buddy, Joshua Jones, and the cops??

I thought I better get a grip on myself, and quit thinking of such bad things. Drew knew where we were, and for some reason he wasn't coming yet. He must have had a reason, and I decided to just wait it out. Drew was a very smart, and a loving father. There may be something more happening outside, which we can't see happening from our location, that he is protecting us from.

I heard more sounds like gun fire, and they were very close this time. I was so glad the girls were still asleep, but for how long I didn't know. Then I heard a thud sound right above us with some yelling. Whatever was happening was right above us in my garage. When will this day be over?

# CHAOS

I fell asleep some time during the night on the mattress next to the girls. I couldn't hear anything more from the outside. The girls were still asleep, which I was concerned about them sleeping this long once I looked at the time on my phone. We had been in the tunnel for over twelve hours already. I knew something was wrong for sure, because Drew wouldn't leave us here if he didn't have to. I wish there was a way to contact him without risking our place of safety. I stood by the wooden door to see if I could get a phone signal, but it was of no use. We would just have to wait, and hope he comes for us soon.

A few hours later Avery started to move around on the mattress, and I knew she was waking up. I whispered that we were in a cave, and we have to be very quiet. I gave her a small flashlight to shine around. She found the stars on the ceiling right away, and then a few of the butterflies. She was happy staying quiet as she explored the cave from the mattress.

Short time later Ansley woke up cranky as all get out. She saw me, and crawled over to my arms whimpering. I could tell she was still groggy from the sedative that had been given to her. I changed her diaper, and fixed her a sippy cup of milk I had cold in the cooler. Opened a few packages of crackers with peanut butter handing them to both girls. They had to be hungry by now. They ate an apple I cut up in small pieces, and a pop tart. They were content with that, and stayed quiet.

Shortly they fell back asleep. I went to the door to see if I could hear anything. It was very quiet outside. I grabbed my phone to text Drew to see if it was safe to come out. When I sent the message I held the phone to the wall in hopes he would get it. No answer back, so I laid back down with the girls. Shortly my phone lit up with a message. I jumped up only to find an answer written in upper case letters, "NO!!".

I laid back down with the girls to wait. It was about an hour later when I heard more gunfire. I knew it was close. Avery woke up wanting to know what the noise was. I told her it was thunder outside, and she laid back down closing her eyes. I sure didn't want her to get scared, and start making any noises. I knew we all needed to be very quiet because we were obviously still in great danger. I still had no idea what was happening outside, and no idea of how long this could go on. I was scared, but I knew we were safe where we were.

Several hours later I heard more sirens, and knew they were right outside my house. I turned on my phone, and Drew had texted that it was now safe to come outside with the girls, but to please cover their eyes. I needed to walk straight towards the house where he would be waiting. Cover their eyes?? I wondered why?? I turned on the lights carefully picking Ansley up to carry her on one hip, and Avery holding my hand walking close to me as we made it up the stairs through the garage to the outside.

The whole back yard was lit up as if it was daylight when it was only around six in the morning. I could see everything fine with the sun starting to rise making things more visible. Police were everywhere with several ambulances standing by with their blue and red lights still swirling around. I scanned the entire backyard for Drew, but couldn't see him anywhere as I managed to slowly walk towards the big house. That was when I saw two lifeless bodies on the ground in puddles of blood. I covered Avery's eyes immediately. She didn't need to see any of this, as I continued searching for Drew. Flashes from cameras were going off as we walked towards the house with people getting too close to us asking me questions. Avery was scared now, and started crying as I told them to please let us through so we could get to the house. Questions I didn't know how to answer, and had no idea why they were even asking me any to begin with. I heard Drew yelling at someone to let him go before I saw him running towards us.

I was so glad to see him as he knelt down to hold

Avery in his arms shielding her from the cameras. I held Ansley close to me covering her face better as Drew grabbed my arm leading us away from everyone. It was complete chaos all around the backyard. There was an ambulance ready to take both girls to the hospital to be checked out, and to see what drugs had been given to them. Drew climbed in with them leaving me standing there by myself. For the first time since coming there I had felt abandoned, and on my own during this horrible crisis. It wasn't the most happiest thought for sure, but I had no one I could turn to. I had a thousand thoughts going off in my head, and feared how the girls lives would change if something bad happens.

I started to walk away when Officer Pete ran to me just before the reporters reached me again. He guided me away from everything, and everyone. Some paramedics came over helping me to sit down on the back of the truck while they checked me out. Everything was a complete daze. I stared at the two lifeless bodies laying on the ground. Two lives were taken, and I didn't know who, or why. All I could hear was this woman telling Officer Pete that I needed to be transported to the hospital immediately. I was in shock. He gently helped me into the ambulance telling me not to worry because everything was going to be fine.

Once at the hospital I was placed in a huge private room where they had taken both girls. Drew rushed over immediately thanking me over and over for keeping his girls safe. All I could do was stare at him. His mouth was moving, but I didn't understand a single word he had been saying. He gave me a hug before he returned back to his girls. I fell asleep after that. I thought maybe it was all a nightmare, and when I woke up everything would be back to normal. But, it wasn't just a nightmare in my head, but a nightmare in real life.

Later that evening, I woke up with Ansley jabbering. I was feeling so much better by then, but didn't move to attract any attention. There was a room full of police officers asking Drew question after question that I just listened in on, to understand what had actually happened. I heard them talking about the dead men being Joshua and Buddy Jones. They were brothers that had planned to kidnap the girls to get ransom money from Drew. Velma was their sister, who had drugged the girls, so they could take them easier, and the girls would be asleep while they drove to Canada. When Buddy and Velma came downstairs to put the girls in the van, the girls were gone from the kitchen with no trace of their whereabouts. The alarm on the door was still on, and neither one had heard the noise it makes when entering or leaving the house. They couldn't figure out where they could have disappeared to. They had even checked my house to see if they were there before they heard the sirens in the distance. I heard that they had hid in my garage for a long time trying to decide on how they were going to escape the area without being caught.

Velma was a big part of the attempted kidnapping by drugging the girls for her brothers. Oh my goodness. How could she do that to the little girls? Vivian and I both knew she was no good from years ago, and we were absolutely right! I had overheard the conversation between Buddy and Velma when I had decided to get the girls out of there. I was thankful my phone never rang to alert Buddy or Velma in the process. It wasn't until I had the girls safe in the cave that it rang with Drew telling me to get them to the cave as soon as possible. Joshua had taken the gun from the bailiff at the courthouse, and start shooting before he was able to escape.

Drew had been grazed by a bullet on his upper arm and shoulder area, but not bad enough to stop him from making sure I had taken his daughters to the cave. He didn't even wait to be looked at by the paramedics before he was on his way to the house. Luckily, the police had arrived first, and had taken him to an area where he would be safe until the threat was over. He could have been injured worse, or he could have jeopardized where I had the girls safely hidden. We all could have been discovered and harmed.

A nurse came in the room putting something in my IV, and I dozed off again. I tried to fight the sleep, but I couldn't. I didn't need to sleep anymore. I needed to eat, and more importantly, I needed to make sure the girls were going to be alright. When I woke up again, the room was dark. I could hear Drew sleeping in the chair on the other side of the room between his girls. I knew he had to have been exhausted over the whole ordeal.

When I woke up the following morning I noticed both girls and Drew were gone. Their beds were stripped, and everything put back to normal waiting to be used by another patient. An aide came in the room, and I asked where the girls and Drew were. She went to find out for me. When she came back she had a nurse with her. I noticed who the nurse was right away, PJ. She was the same one who gave me trouble when I had delivered Avery. Once she looked at me, she recognized me as well. A few snickers came from her, which surprised the young aide, but not me. PJ right away said she would have ordered me a late breakfast, but the kitchen was closed, so the workers could only get a few lunch items that were already prepared. Either I would have to wait until around one in the afternoon, or I could eat a cup of fruit they had in at the nurse's station. I gladly accepted the cup of fruit thanking her kindly. She sent the aide to retrieve it.

Before the aide was able to get back to the room, PJ had informed me that she remembered me. I had been the one who caused her to get in trouble with her superior, and she was removed from the labor and delivery ward to a different area. I just looked at her deciding I had nothing to say to her. When the aide brought me the fruit cup, PJ left the room. I asked the young aide when PJ's shift would be over. When she informed me not until midnight, I let out a groan of distaste. I would have to put up with PJ popping in and out for another twelve hours. I knew one thing though, I did not need anything to 'help me sleep' today, and I was going to make sure I didn't get anything more.

After dinner had been served that night, PJ came in smiling from ear to ear. I asked her where the girls were. She made a sinister laugh telling me they were now with their mother. I about jumped from my bed. I asked her to repeat what she had said, and she did. When I asked her what had happened, all she could do was smile as she laughed, and said the girls didn't need me any longer now. I was shocked that they were gone. She quickly told me she had a shot for me to help me sleep better through the night. I told her I didn't need anything, but she grabbed the IV tube injecting it before walking out. I had to stop it from entering my body. I needed to get out of there, so I pinched the tube tightly shut while I removed the needle from my arm.

I must not have pinched it tight enough, or soon enough to keep the sedative from entering my body because I was asleep for a few hours. When I finally woke up it was pitch black in my room, as well as outside. I needed to get away, and get away from there quickly. I did my best to protect the girls, and now they were with their mom. How could this have happened? I needed to tell Drew how sorry I was. I couldn't believe what could have happened for them to be with their mom now. Their mom was dead, and now they were, too. I had to get back to the house, and the only way I could do that was to walk there.

I got up to get dressed finding that all my clothes were gone, even my cell phone. I only had on the hospital gown with their skid free socks on my feet. I quietly opened my door seeing a dimly lit hallway without a single nurse at the station. The stairs were right across from my room, and I quickly went down them to the outside without being caught. As I started to walk towards the house, I noticed how warm it was for being that late at night.

The more I walked, the more I thought about little Avery and Ansley being gone. I know I had heard Ansley earlier jabbering when the police officers were talking to Drew, and she sounded fine to me then. Had I dreamed that? Was it something that happened later? What could have happened? Avery had been watching a cartoon on her little notepad. I cried so much as I walked along the streets. Several times people stopped asking if I was alright. I ignored them, and continued to walk through the town to the outskirts. How could they ask me such a stupid question when I was dressed in a hospital gown, crying, and a complete mess. I felt my heart had been ripped from my chest with the girls gone. I couldn't have helped them any more than I had when I retrieved them from the kitchen. The little girls were so special to me. So very special.

My feet were starting to hurt while walking on the sidewalks so I walked as much in the grass as I could. I was starting to get cold even though the night air was very warm, but I had to reach the house. I just had to!! The town started to fade behind me after several hours of walking. I wanted to stop to rest, but I knew I couldn't. Not yet. I had to get to the house. That was my only determination I had at the moment. I thought of all the things I had done with the girls, with Vivian, and also with Drew. All my happy memories were now nothing, but sadness. Was I being punished for the things I had done as a child? I began to wonder. I had never meant to hurt anyone ever, but my mother had told me that someday I would get the karma I deserved. Was it this? It had to have been. I was just a rotten person through and through just like I had been told as a kid.

I came to the corn field that was in front of the big house. I would make it after all. I decided to cut through the corn field to get me to the house quicker. The ground was so cold, but it wasn't like I had expected it to be. My feet were really hurting bad, but I was almost there. I didn't think I would ever make through that corn field. The stalks were so high I couldn't see anything, but knew I had to be getting close. The corn stalks were constantly swatting my face as I walked on, leaving scratches that stung with my tears flowing down. I finally made it through the corn field to where I was standing in front of the driveway to Drew's house.

I fell into the ditch scrapping my legs and arms with the thorns from the branches of blackberry bushes that grew wild along the road. I didn't care. I was home. Or was I? I pressed the code for the gate to open, and nothing happened. I pressed it several more times, and still it didn't move. Drew must have changed the code already.

Sunrise was beginning to peak to begin another beautiful morning. Not a beautiful morning as far as I was concerned. I was drained, and slowly slid down the side of the wall that held the gate secure. The warm sun sure felt good on my skin from being out all night. I drifted off to sleep leaning against that wall. It wasn't too long when thought I had heard a car coming down the road. I couldn't raise my hand up to get their attention to stop. I heard it slowing down, and before I knew it, it had turned into the driveway. It was Mark and Carolyn coming to the house. When Mark opened the window to press the code for the gate I heard Carolyn gasp, telling Mark to get Drew from the house immediately as she jumped out the car running to me. She put her arms around me as I clung on to her telling her over and over I was so sorry. My tears were falling down my face as I repeated those four words over and over. Carolyn told me I had nothing to be sorry for. I wasn't able to understand why she could say that when her granddaughters were dead. Dead, all because of me!

I heard another car pull up. It was Drew this time running to me. Carolyn said I needed an ambulance immediately, and to get the blanket from the backseat of his car. He called 911 while grabbing the blanket so Carolyn could drape it over me. I reached for his hand telling him I was so sorry for everything between my heavy sobs. He was assuring me everything was alright, and soon the ambulance would be there to take me to the hospital. I didn't want to go back there I had told them, I said "no hospital" over and over.

I could hear the ambulance siren in the distance, and before I knew what was happening, I had been loaded into the ambulance, and on my way to the hospital. Carolyn rode in the ambulance with me holding my hand. I told her again and again how sorry I was as I cried. She said I had nothing to be sorry for. I cried out that I did. The girls were dead because I didn't protect them good enough. I should have protected them better, but I didn't. Carolyn looked at me whispering that the girls weren't dead, they were still at home probably sleeping in their beds.

I looked at her puzzled as I told her that PJ had told me they were now with their mother. Vivian was dead, and if they were with her, they were dead, too. Carolyn shook her head saying they were fine, and that I had protected them one hundred per cent perfectly. Everyone was very happy I was there to take them out of the house when I had, and to the cave keeping them safe. PJ didn't know what she was talking about. Carolyn hugged me telling me I was a true hero keeping their granddaughters safe like I had.

We got to the hospital within minutes. Seemed like it took me forever to walk it just hours ago. Drew had met us there, and rushed over to me. Carolyn told him what I had told her in the ambulance adding that he needed to do something about that PJ saying such a horrible thing to me.

I asked Carolyn to please stay with me for awhile. I didn't trust them at the hospital. I didn't want to be there. Several nurses came in to clean me up from my blooded face, arms, and legs. I was given a clean gown to put on. Carolyn helped me remove the soiled gown, and get the clean one on me. When they removed the socks off my feet, I heard Carolyn gasp in horror at what she had seen. My feet were cut up pretty bad, I had many blisters that had ruptured with pus coming out already, and were swollen double the size that they should be. Every time the nurse tried to gently wipe the bottoms of my feet, I had winched in pain.

They put another IV in my arm, and was going to put another injection in for the pain. I told them they needed to get away from me, and I fought them with every ounce of strength I had in me. I was not going to have any injection for the pain. I wasn't going to be put asleep again like PJ had kept doing to me earlier.

Drew was back in my cubicle with the head of the hospital, Jeffrey Johnsen, with him. Drew asked me to tell him what had happened to me, and to answer a few questions, if I could. I told the man that PJ told me the girls had gone to be with their mother, she had kept me sedated too much, and I couldn't get anyone there to help me. Jeffrey asked how I got to the house where I had been found outside Drew's gate. I told him I walked there. Drew added that it was over ten miles to his house. Jeffrey asked why it upset me so much that the girls had gone to be with their mother. I started crying so hard while I told him it was because their mother was dead. The look on his face was one which I will never forget. He shook his head asking if I remembered who the nurse was. I replied PJ, which I had already told him several times before. I wondered if he had been really listening or just hearing words so he could cover this up in his records on me.

Jeffrey excused himself asking Drew to walk out with him. I was still in ear shot of hearing what they were saying. I had to admit it didn't sound good for PJ. Drew said that Jeffrey better do something quick about this, and with that nurse PJ, because he was representing me, and making it known loud and clear that there would definitely be a lawsuit filed immediately as he was walking away. Jeffrey tried to calm Drew down saying there had to be some explanation as to why PJ would have said something like that. Great, he didn't believe me. I figured about that much, and I wanted out of this place NOW!! Drew turned around asking if the nurses could say whatever they want to their patients, without any regards for a patients feelings? Drew repeated himself with the words **IMMEDIATELY** emphasized while he was walking away.

When he walked back to me in my cubicle, he told me how sorry he was that I had to go through that. He assured me the girls were absolutely fine, and both were at home with his dad and Susan. Avery has been asking about me nonstop, and Ansley has been calling for me. He was sorry he had taken my clothes, but he was going to bring me some clean clothes back when visiting hours started today.

Susan, his sister, was already at the house since yesterday to help until their parents had arrived. His parents had shortened their vacation in the Bahamas to get to Drew's house once they were aware what had happened concerning the Jones brothers. They were on their way there to help out with the girls, and everything else Drew might need. That was when his parents had pulled in the driveway finding me at the wall by the gate.

I looked at him asking if the girls were really fine. He shook his head yes that they were, adding I will be too, soon. I told him I was so happy to hear that news. I also told him I didn't want to stay at the hospital. I wanted to go to my house. I didn't trust them there, because they kept giving me drugs. He said he would see about getting me out of there. Carolyn said she'd be more than happy to help me at the house with whatever I needed. Drew asked me if that would be alright with me, and I nodded it would. She was a retired nurse herself, and I knew I could trust her. I said that would make me extremely happy.

As soon as I was discharged from the hospital, we were on our way home. The emergency doctor had given Carolyn the instructions I needed for my scrapes, and especially for my feet. My feet were pretty infected. They would require the most attention, and that I needed to stay off them for at least two weeks. He apologized for everything that had happened to me while there, as we were getting ready to leave. I just looked at him without uttering a single word.

Drew drove me straight to my house. While Carolyn ran in to get my bed ready for me, Drew scooped me into his arms to carry me into my bedroom, then he excused himself. Carolyn helped me out of that hospital gown, and into my own pajamas. A few minutes after getting settled in the bed, I heard Drew walking on the porch towards my bedroom arcadia door. Carolyn announced I had visitors. Drew had brought the girls to see me. Avery ran over to me stopping short at the edge of the bed to stare at me. I could tell she was scared. I never thought of what I looked like with all the scratches all over my face, and arms. I told her I was so glad to see her. She then decided to climb on the bed scooting close, and asked me if my boo boos hurt. She gently touched my arms giving them a kiss to help with the healing. Ansley was scared to death when she saw me, and not wanting to come any closer than necessary. She hung on to Drew with a grip he couldn't pry her from. I understood, and just said, "hi baby girl". She then smiled, and wanted me to hold her. I held both girls in my arms while crying telling them I was so glad to see them. I was so glad Drew had brought them down to see me. So very glad!!

# A Time to Heal

<hr>

Early the next morning at the butt crack of dawn, Drew was knocking at my arcadia door holding a tray full of food for me. I motioned for him to come in. I didn't hesitate to eat my breakfast when he set it on the bed. I was pretty hungry, but I did offer some of it to Drew. He smiled saying that he had already eaten. It didn't take me long to wolf down that breakfast. I noticed where his arm was wrapped in a bandage. It had to have been where he was grazed by a bullet. He came pretty close to having that bullet penetrate his shoulder-arm area. He noticed that I was looking at it, saying that's what happens when you stand where the police tell you not to stand with a small chuckle. I gently touched it. You could tell it was sore from the way his face crinkled up. He said it was more sore than anything else, but I knew it was more than that. Okay Drew, I thought, you can be the big brave guy here if you want. He had every right to be with everything he had been through.

In between bites, I asked Drew whatever became of Velma. I had known the ending results with the Jones boys, but no one said anything about Velma. Drew told me that Velma had been telling the police officers that the Jones brothers had tied her up in the house. She had been tied to a chair in the kitchen, but it was only a ploy in their scheme of keeping her out of their plans, and getting her into trouble. Once her brothers had been shot dead, she ran to their van, taking off as fast as she could to get away from there. She had lost control of the van while turning onto the main road going at such a high rate of speed. That's where she went in the deep ditch, hit a culvert, and the van flipped in the air throwing her out the window. Velma had died from the accident immediately from severe head trauma she had received.

I wasn't glad Velma had died the way she had, but I also was happy she had died at the same time. I didn't know she had confessed to the police officers in the house questioning her on everything before taking off like she had, until Drew told me. It answered many of the other questions I had about Velma's role in everything.

Drew told me not to worry about the brothers, or her any longer. It was over, and we were all safe, which was the most important thing in Drew's mind. We all needed some time to heal, and we will heal from this whole traumatic ordeal. He was sure of that. He sat on the edge of the bed taking my hand into his to tell me how grateful he was that I had gotten the girls out safely, and in the nick of time. He continued by saying there was no way he could ever repay me for everything I had done for him. He said I was so brave with everything happening right outside my house at the end, and not giving up our safe location.

I told him I didn't know exactly what had been happening outside, but I had thought for sure I had heard gun shots often. Avery had asked what that noise was, and I had to lie by telling her it had been thunder that we were hearing. The girls had been drugged up enough to sleep through most of the commotion. The three of us stayed on the mattress most of the time while everything was happening outside, trying to remain very quiet.

I told him I felt like a fool for reacting the way I had when PJ had said, "the girls were with their mother now". I had thought I had done a great job….Drew shushed me from going on any further. He told me I had done an excellent job, and in the condition I had been in at that time, he would have reacted the exact same way if PJ had told him that as well. I was not to worry about that, not about my current condition, and what I had looked, or sounded like from now on. We all need to think positive, and look for happiness in the future. Happiness in the future….right. I will never forget what had happened that day for the rest of my life!

Drew also stated that he was going to represent me in the lawsuit against the hospital, and PJ. No one, but no one deserved to be treated, or spoken to in that way after going through pure hell like I had been through. A hospital is suppose to help people, not send patients over the edge like PJ had done to me. I just nodded my head in agreement, and whispered a thank you.

We heard Carolyn coming to check on me, and Drew said we would talk more about everything later. I needed my medication, and the bandages around my feet changed right now. Carolyn came in smiling at us saying she could come back at a later time if we needed her to, with a wink to Drew. I said she was fine being there, and to please come in.

When she carefully unwrapped my feet, I thought I was going to pass out from the intense pain. Carolyn was being as gentle as she could, but the pain was more than I could handle. Drew's eyes bulged when he saw the bottom of my feet saying he needed to take a picture of my feet for the up coming lawsuit, as evidence. I was sure they looked horrid, but I felt Drew knew what he was doing. That was when I got to see exactly what the bottom of my feet looked like for myself. Drew handed me his phone, and I gasped out loud bringing my hand to my mouth. They looked like raw hamburger meat to me, from the tip of my toes all the way to my heals. Carolyn totally agreed, but added that they would heal in time, and everyday I would experience less and less pain. I hope she's right! That was a picture I will never be able to erase from my mind!

After Carolyn cleaned my feet, put the ointment on before wrapping them again, she told me the entire family was going to be over for the traditional Saturday cook out. She was checking to see if I would feel up to it to be there as well. If I didn't feel up to being there, the family would completely understand. I said I would love to be there, as long as there isn't any hamburgers being grilled, and the three of us laughed together. All I could think of was food, and getting this all behind me.

Drew added that he had picked up a wheelchair in town earlier in the morning for me to get around in, and he would be back in plenty of time to put me in it to take me up to the patio, since I had to stay off my feet. They started spouting off rules of things that I could, and couldn't do next. I gave them a two finger salute while smiling. Drew said they also had a foot tub with a jet stream at the house that in two, or maybe in three more days, depending on how much the feet have healed, that I would be using. Carolyn said my feet will love that, but until then, I was not to be putting any pressure on them by standing. I was to stay off my feet completely. I assured her that I intended to do that, because I wanted get better soon. I didn't want to be waited on, and would do whatever it took to get back on my feet as soon as possible. With that being said, Drew excused himself so he could get everything ready for the cook out. Carolyn added that she had already made a pasta salad, had her special baked beans in the oven already, and had the steaks marinating in the refrigerator.

After Drew left, Carolyn sat with me talking mostly about getting me better. Then she started crying telling me how much she had appreciated me making sure her precious granddaughters were safely hidden with me in this cave we have talked so much about. She now understood about why it was important to get the girls ready for a possible cave visit. I told her that they were my number one priority when the whole thing had happened. I told her that both Vivian and I didn't trust Velma for some reason. We just couldn't put our finger on as to why, but our gut feelings were spot on.

I continued telling Carolyn that I was glad to have been able to help when I was needed. Carolyn said I have helped the family in more ways than one way. First, it was to help Vivian and Drew be the family they wanted so desperately, and then saving the same little girls from something that could have been so terrible to even think about. She hugged me telling me I would always be loved by them, and always be a part of their family. That made me feel so good hearing it from her. She was such a wonderful person that was kind to me, **all** the time.

We watched an early morning movie together before she had to get back to the house. I understood, and decided I needed to get some rest myself. I hadn't done anything in a few days, but I sure was tired enough to fall asleep fast. I could faintly hear the cars pulling into the driveway knowing the time was getting closer for the cookout to begin, but continued to sleep a little longer.

Once I finally woke up I noticed on the clock that it was almost two. I must have been really tired! I sat up immediately reaching for the clothes set out by Carolyn, before she went back to the house earlier. I changed into them as fast as I could. I didn't know how long it would be before someone would be there to get me, but I wanted to be ready.

Drew brought the wheelchair with him when he came to pick me up. Avery was riding in it while laughing all the way, and yelling for her daddy to go faster. She was enjoying the ride so much that I hated for her to have to give it up for me to sit in. When they got to the porch Avery jumped off running inside to see me, while Drew wheeled it into the house. Drew came in my bedroom asking if I was ready to eat, as my chariot was waiting. I nodded that I sure was. He easily scooped me up into his arms, and carried me to the wheel chair putting me in it ever so gently.

Avery jumped onto my lap, and rode with me up to the patio. When I looked to the patio I could do nothing, but stare at everything. There was this huge banner hanging from the house that said, "Our hero, Allison, thank you and we LOVE you!!". It was all I could do to keep the tears back. The closer we got to the patio everyone started standing up clapping their hands while looking at me. Susan was the first to yell "We love you Allison". As soon as Drew had wheeled me on the patio, everyone came over to thank me for what I had done, and congratulated me. I couldn't explain that I was only doing what they would have done, but they had said they wouldn't have been that brave. They said it took someone very brave to do it, and that special person was me. I saw other people there as well, and they were the people that worked for Drew. I told everyone they were all so kind, but I didn't need this recognition. They all shouted that I certainly did.

Wow! I said two lies within one week. I had said that I didn't deserve all this, but deep down I was so happy that they had thought I should. I had done something good in my life once again, and I had to admit, it felt good. My feet were hurting, but deep inside me, I felt good!

Drew walked over to me holding a small box wrapped in his hands. It was a little token of the love from everyone to always remember what I had done for every single one of them, and to remember that I am family. I was dearly loved by all. I truly felt their love for me right then, as I was being careful unwrapping it. Avery said she hoped it was a new doll. I had to laugh with everyone over that expression from an almost four year old.

It wasn't a doll, but it was the most beautiful heart shaped necklace with the girls names engraved on each side of a large diamond in the center. I placed my shaky hand over my heart as I thanked everyone. Drew took it out of the box, and as I held my hair up, he put it around my neck clasping it shut. It was so beautiful. A few of the guys remarked that Drew definitely had good taste when it came to picking out jewelry. There was no doubt about that, Drew surely did have great taste in jewelry.

Avery broke the emotional feelings of everyone by asking if we were going to eat now. She said her belly was hungry. Carolyn, Drew and I said that it was time, unless it was 'raw hamburger meat' together. No one knew what we were talking about, and we were the only three laughing over our little inside joke that we had. There was so much food on the tables with plenty of steaks ready to be devoured. I brought two pillows from the house with me so I could rest my feet on them, and not on the patio flagstone where I might accidentally stand up. Drew picked me up from my wheel chair placing me on the bench at the table. Ansley sat to my left in her high chair so I could help her when her grandmothers were eating. They had been keeping her occupied all day, and I felt they could use a break. Ansley was always such a happy baby that it made it easy.

Later that night when everyone was getting ready to leave I thanked them all once again. So many gave me a hug upon their departure, with several of them kissing my cheek. Almost everyone had left, with everything cleaned up, and put away. It wore Avery and Ansley out, and they fell asleep almost immediately after their baths. The older kids were busy trying to catch lightning bugs along the edge of the yard in jars.

Drew had started a fire in the fire pit, making the rest of the night pleasantly nice. Carolyn was the first to ask about this cave again that Avery and Drew had talked so much about. Drew said I had the honors in telling them about it, how I found it, how he rewired it, and how I supplied things for it, just in case we would ever need it. Where it was located was the most asked question. I told them about finding it by chance while trying to relocate my treadmill in my basement, and that there was a tunnel from the main house to my little house all underground. I went into every last detail about it. It had been elaborately built some time ago, and disguised with a canning jar shelf hiding the entrance. Of course they wanted to see it, so Drew said at a later date we would definitely show them.

I finished with the question and answer session saying that I thought it could have been part of the Underground Railroad, but no one at the library had any information on the house. They had information on other homes in the area, but this one wasn't listed. The latest information the librarian could find, was where the house now sits was nothing but an empty field.

That was when Mark said that he remembered finding some very old papers in the attic on the house when Drew and Vivian had purchased it. He said if no one had removed those papers, that they might still be there. He was interested in finding them now just to see if this property was holding some significant historical information. If he remembered correctly there was also a ledger-like book among those papers. How cool that could be if there was information on the house that was attached to the Underground Railroad.

Drew and Carolyn took me back to my place once the talk on the house had subsided, and everyone else had left. Drew was so gentle carrying me into my house. I thought I could get use to this pretty easy. Carolyn folded the wheel chair in half carrying it into the house, so I could use it inside if I needed to. I thought that would be nice to have inside, so I could use it to go to the bathroom without having to have help all the time.

Carolyn removed the bandages off my feet to clean off the nasty stuff, apply fresh ointment, and fresh bandages. She commented that they were still pretty infected, and that maybe tomorrow we should let the air get to them for awhile. I nodded that it sounded good to me.

I thanked them for everything that day, and how much it had meant to me. I loved the necklace very much, and agreed that Drew did have very good taste in jewelry. Carolyn said he always picked out the most unique, and beautiful pieces of jewelry since he was a little kid. All Drew could do was grunt calling out a 'Mom'. Carolyn laughed giving me a wink as she hugged me good night, and headed out the door.

After she was gone, I told Drew that I thought his mom was right, because it was a very beautiful piece of jewelry. He was glad I liked it. I told him I didn't like it…. I loved it. It was a very thoughtful gift. He gave me a good-night hug before leaving that lingered a little longer than normal, but I didn't mind. Nope, I didn't mind it one bit.

Drew said a reporter wanted to do a story for the town newspaper on us, about what we had gone through. I really didn't want to relive that awful day. I told Drew I wasn't sure I wanted to do it, but Drew thought that the community needed to know the facts, and not what they were speculating that had happened. I asked if he was going to be there, and he shook his head yes. So, I agreed to it. The reporter was scheduled to come to the house in three days, if I was up to it. If I wasn't ready, the reporter would have to wait until I was.

I was glad when the interview was over. The reporter was very kind, and sympathetic when asking questions, knowing it was still a very delicate subject matter, and horrible situation we had gone through. Several pictures had been taken during the whole ordeal that day, as well as right there in Drew's house then. Before the interviewer had left, he said to give him a few days to write it all up before it would appear in the newspaper. Whew, I was glad when he had left. Rehashing every detail had brought back some ugly thoughts of that day that I had preferred to forget.

That night as I laid in my bed, I thought of everything that had happened. But, my mind kept going back to the hug Drew had just given me. I tried not to put any extra thought into it, but it kept returning. Was I out of line, thinking it had meant more than just a simple good-night hug? I wasn't sure, but I know I enjoyed it. I embarrassingly enjoyed it very much, and I also enjoyed it whenever Drew is around. Oh dear, I had to stop thinking this way about Drew. He was my best friend's husband. Even though Vivian is no longer alive, I wasn't sure what she would have thought of me having these thoughts of Drew. Vivian, his parents, siblings, and even Vivian's family might not like it one iota. That could cause me grief down the road.

The next morning, Carolyn was at the door bright and early with the foot tub in her hands. She filled it with lukewarm water from the sink adding some Epsom salts to dissolve in it. I removed the bandages carefully for her, and looked at the bottoms of my feet. They looked disgusting, and had a rotten stench to them. I sat on the edge of the bed slowly immersing my feet in the water. Oh the pain from just the water touching them was horrible. Carolyn switched on the jets to get the water to bubble up. After a few minutes it started to feel better on my feet.

After a good half hour of my feet soaking and enjoying the bubbly water, I took them out patting them dry like Carolyn had showed me how to do. Some bad skin had peeled off already. The part of new skin was dark pink in color, but it didn't hurt. I was glad of that! I was determined to get my feet heeled quickly. I asked Carolyn what she thought about putting aloe vera on my feet. I had some growing in a pot on the back porch next to my rocker that we could use. She thought it would be fine, and went out to snip off a piece. We peeled the outer layer back of the aloe vera applying the gooey insides right onto my feet. At first it didn't feel very good at all, but shortly my feet quit burning, and a cool sensation of heeling was felt. Carolyn carefully bandaged my feet so I wouldn't smear the aloe vera on anything.

Several days had gone by without much happening. I was bored out of my mind. I needed something to happen. I had put all the jigsaw puzzles together from the house, played more than enough solitaire with the cards, watched more movies than necessary, and colored many many pictures with Avery.

Then Carolyn came down holding the newspaper under her arm. I knew immediately what it had in it, "the story of the year", as Carolyn had announced. I didn't open it until after she had left, in case it upset me. I didn't want to be upset in front of her when it had been Drew's idea that we should do the interview in the first place. I carefully unfolded the newspaper exposing the front page, and there we were. It was as if it had jumped right out at me. The pictures were very detailed. One had me carrying Ansley in my arms with Avery glued right to my side, with my hand shielding her eyes. I was staring down at the dead bodies on the ground, with a look of horror on my face as I walked past them. I shook seeing that photo, and decided to read the story later. It was only about two minutes when I decided I needed to read the complete story after all. I had to admit, that reporter had done a wonderful job writing it. I finished reading it, and put it on top of the night stand. I decided to take a nap for awhile.

My feet were finally heeled within the two weeks like the doctor had said. The doctor said I could now walk around a little. I didn't think they would ever get better, but I honestly think they had gotten better because of the aloe vera we had been applying. After applying that gooey stuff, it hadn't taken too long to heal. Carolyn was getting ready to go back home in a few days. I will miss her for sure. She had helped me with everything I needed during the time she was there.

Drew was down to see me everyday like clock work. He'd sit and chat with me for hours. I enjoyed his visits. The day I was finally allowed to be on my feet, I walked up to the house when I heard him pull in the driveway. He was glad I was able to get up, and out of my house on my own. I wasn't sure if that meant he was tired of picking me up to put in my wheel chair, that he was tired of coming down to my house, or genuinely just happy for me. Either way, I was happy to be walking on my own accord.

Often I would go to the house to assist Carolyn with the girls during the day. When the girls were down for their naps in the afternoon, the two of us would sit on the patio to chat. She would tell me all about raising her kids, the many places they had traveled to, and just life in general. I told her a little about my life, without going in to many deep details. I didn't think there was any need to tell her everything. I'm sure she knew more than what she ever let on anyhow.

Carolyn had been busy in the kitchen for several days preparing many meals to freeze for Drew and the girls, for when she was back at her own home. She didn't want him to have to cook after spending the day at work, or in court. I didn't have the heart to tell her she didn't have to do that because I could prepare their meals now.

When Mark arrived to take her back home, he noticed all the meals she had in the freezer for Drew, and commented on the fact that he didn't have any meals in the freezer for himself, as he winked at me. I knew he was teasing her, but she said Drew only knew how to grill. I chuckled at that. It was true that he was a great grill master, but I also knew he was very capable of cooking meals in the kitchen as well. I knew that for a fact. I think she was just trying to help him out all she could. Do the motherly thing for her son and granddaughters.

After Mark and Carolyn left to go home, Drew asked if I felt up to a trip to the zoo with the girls the following weekend. I was more than ready to get away from the house. I hadn't been anywhere other than to the doctors office for the past three weeks. Avery was excited about those plans. Ansley mocked Avery's excitement. Drew thought it would be better to celebrate Ansley's birthday on the quieter side after everything we had been through. I couldn't agree more. His parents, siblings, and Vivian's parents would be there on Sunday for some cake and ice cream, after a grilled meal of course.

Drew had the girls back in the day care center once Carolyn was gone. I kept busy during the mornings at my job, and on my treadmill in the afternoon for two hours. I knew when Drew would be arriving home with the girls after work, and I would walk up to the house to warm up what he had put out to thaw on the counter, and place in the microwave for him. Tonight it was stuffed peppers, and I had to admit, they smelled delicious! I usually stayed for dinner, and cleaned up afterwards while Drew played with the girls outside until it was time for their bath, and bedtime.

That zoo weekend was here quicker than what I was ready for. I dug out my old sneakers to wear, hoping my feet would be able to handle all the walking we would be doing. I would push through the walk the best I could without complaining. No whining from me!

Drew had the car packed up with the girls ready and excited to go to the zoo. I grabbed my bag, and got in the car. Once at the zoo, I asked Drew if he brought sunscreen for the girls. He hadn't thought of that. I smiled as I pulled a spray can out of my bag applying it on the girls. I told him he might want to put some on his neck, and face because I was sure they'd get sunburned. I went to spray some on the back of my neck, and he took the can away from me spraying it on for me. He rubbed it in so gently. I thanked him, and took the can to spray my face, and arms myself.

We had a great day looking at all the animals, eating the lunch Drew had packed, and watching the girls feed the baby animals in the petting area. Avery wanted to bring a little goat home with us. Drew said maybe when they got a little older they could have a small pet. She was happy with that information, and I can tell you, she'll remind him of what he said for weeks to come.

We didn't even make it home before they were sound asleep in the backseat. Drew looked at me wanting to know if I could go for a Dairy Queen treat. Anything cold would have been fine with me. He ordered a banana split for himself, so I decided on a blizzard, a large turtle pecan one at that. Was so glad I did. It hit the spot, and was so delicious.

At the house Drew carried Avery upstairs to her bedroom, and I carried Ansley to hers. I was able to get her diaper changed, and her pajamas on by the time Drew came in to kiss her goodnight. He stood next to me looking at her in the crib with sadness in his eyes. He whispered that both girls are growing up too quick for him, and wished they'd remain small longer. I had to agree. It doesn't seem possible Ansley was turning one the next day, and Avery will be four years old in a few more months. He put his arm around me giving me a sideways hug. I put my arm around his waist hugging him back.

I know in time, the girls are going to start questioning things. How Drew decides to answer those questions will be up to him. When the girls get old enough to put two and two together, and realize Ansley's birth date is a few months **after** the death of their mother, that will be the day Drew would need his answers ready.

# And Then It Happened

---

Much time has passed since that whole ordeal had happened at the house, but my mind often goes back to that day when I least expect it to. It was as if there was a reason I wasn't to forget what I had seen, had heard, and had gone through that dreadful day. I got on with my life the best I could, and Drew continued asking me to come to the house for dinners frequently. I enjoyed being with Drew and the girls very much. It wasn't going to be long before Avery was starting kindergarten. Ansley was growing like a bad weed learning so many things. That didn't seem possible, but life has a way of moving on regardless how much you wish it to stop, or at least slow down.

Drew seems as if he has accepted things the way they are now, too. I know he still misses Vivian a great deal, and we all go to visit her at the cemetery on most weekends. Sometimes I go over to just sit to chat with her, getting things off my mind, and letting her know her girls are growing up so fast, and miss her. I talk as if she was right next to me like we had done in the past. It may seem rather crazy to do, but it is a help to me.

Vivian's parents still have the girls come for a weekend, but it is now only once a month. In time I think that will become a thing of the past as well. Drew's parents are thinking about moving closer to him, which I think would be very nice for all of them. So many changes happening. Life really did need to slow down for me!!

Drew was invited to a friend's wedding one Saturday evening in town, and asked if I'd be his plus one. I agreed to go with him to both the wedding, and the reception. My circle of friends still hadn't grown much past the family, and Drew's people in his office. Just to be out of the house always felt good.

I dressed myself to the nines for this wedding by buying myself a beautiful dress with shoes to match. Drew even complimented me on how nice I looked when he picked me up at my house. Several times when we were stopped for a red light, he'd look over at me with this crazy smile across his face. If I could only read his mind!

The wedding was absolutely beautiful, and the reception was fantastic as most are. At least as far as I knew since it was the first wedding I had attended. I sat with Drew until a guy came over asking me to dance with him. I saw Drew go hang out at the bar talking with some other guys there while drinking his adult beverages while I was busy dancing and having a great time. Several times I saw the whole group at the bar turn at the exact same time to look at me. I wondered what was going on in their conversations for them all to turn to look at the same time. I kept my eyes on them while I danced the night away. I had never had so many men ask me to dance before, and I was enjoying every second of it.

I watched Drew basically drink the night away, one right after another, and knew that wasn't like him. He would enjoy some beers now and then, but these weren't beers he was chugging down. The reception was dwindling down, and the disc jockey announced final dance, and it was ladies choice. Finally!! I walked over to Drew asking if he'd like to dance. His eyes were so blood shot red, and he grumbled something I didn't hear very well. But, he did dance with me, and it was very nice dancing with him when he wasn't losing his balance. Before the music was over, he abruptly stopped dancing stating that we were leaving. I looked at him, and he repeated we were leaving, adding a **now** to it. Huh!! I wanted to finish the dance, but he was extremely irritable about something, so I hastily grabbed my purse leaving without him uttering a single word the entire drive home. He was upset about something, and I thought it was a good idea for me to not ask any questions at this time.

Once we got to the house he jumped out of his car immediately telling me to get out. I got out of the car, and out of the garage, before he said I needed to be out of the house, too. He gave me five whole days to get moved out. He was shouting all this to me as if the whole neighborhood had to know what he was saying. I stood there like a stone statue watching him stagger, and barely making it into his house, slamming the door shut. What had just happened?

I was so confused as to what had set him off like that. I tried to say something, but he never stopped to listen to me. I stood there for several seconds shaking my head in bewilderment. Everything had been fine before the wedding, and then wham, it was a scene like from some Dr. Jekyll and Mr. Hyde movie. I walked to my place thinking about what had just happened, and what did I do wrong. I knew it must have been something I did, but what was it? I needed to find out. I was sick to my stomach of what it could have been. I opened the door to my house thinking I will make every effort to be out of his house in five days, since that was what he wanted me to do.

Was I hurt? Yes, most definitely I was hurt. I quickly changed into my pajamas, and found a few empty tubs I could put some of my things into right away. I hadn't packed much when I had decided it could all wait until morning. I cried myself to sleep thinking how such a wonderful night had turned into me being evicted from my house, and my heart breaking.

Around three in the morning there was someone pounding loudly on my front door. I wasn't going to answer it at that time of night, but the pounding got louder, and louder. It was Drew shouting at the top of his lungs to please open the door. Great! Just what I needed, a drunk to lambaste me with some more crap. I jerked the door open for him to come in. He stepped inside telling me he was very sorry for what he had said, and how he had acted earlier. He had time to think things over, and to sober up a little as well. He asked me to please not move out when he saw that I had a tub already packed. I listened to him explain how wrong it was of him to talk to me like that, and began to say how sorry he was. How he had acted and the things he had said stung yet, and I wasn't going to let him off the hook that easy. I was heartbroken, and I was going to let him know how much he had hurt me with his words, and actions.

I looked him squarely in the eyes telling him to give one good reason for me to stay when he had made it loud and clear that I had five days to be out. I wasn't speaking to him in the kindest way or voice either. He deserved it after everything he had said earlier. He grabbed me by my shoulders saying, "for the girls sake". Wow, he pulled on the one thing that he knew that would hurt me the most. I looked at him in a disgusted way, and said to give me a better reason than bringing his daughters into his mess. He let out a deep sigh, saying he needed me there. Needed me?? Anyone could do what I have done for him since arriving there. I told him I was glad he felt he **"needed me"** as sarcastic as I could possibly muster, as if I was someone who would jump when he said to. My eyes were filling with tears before he finally let out another deep sigh telling me I had to stay........ he was in love with me pulling me into his arms before planting his lips on to mine.

When he was pulling his lips off mine, I looked into his deep green eyes. I whispered, "you love me?". He replied that he loved me very much. When he saw me dancing with all the guys that night at the reception, he was worried he was going to lose me, and he went into a fit of jealousy. The angrier he got, the more he drank. To make matters worse was that he had drank too much, and was a mess. I told him all he had to have done was ask me to dance with him, and I would have. He gazed into my eyes saying he owed me a dance big time, so I had to stick around to collect that dance from him. I grabbed the collar of his shirt on both sides pulling him towards me, so I was able to kiss him. After several kisses that grew deeper in passion with each one, he scooped me into his arms carrying me to my bed. Gently he put me down on the bed as he started to caress me with his hands. I was able to remove his shirt before he took over removing everything else in record speed.

I had never been with a man before, and I now know what I had been missing out on all these years being single and dateless. It was the most amazing night for me as we made love over, and over until our bodies couldn't do it any longer. I knew I was in love with Drew months ago, but never thought of him being in love with me. That night was the most spectacular moment of my life. We both fell asleep until late morning. I was still resting my head on his chest when I woke up. As soon as I moved to get up, Drew woke up, pulling me back to him kissing me more.

Drew said we needed to talk about last night. I didn't want to talk about it. I thought it was the most perfect night of my life, and I didn't want that memory to be tarnished in any way. I was worried he had been too drunk, and now after being sober that he thought maybe he had made a big mistake making love to me. It had been the most beautiful loving experience ever for me, and I didn't need it to be wiped away as a "mistake" with the excuse that he had been drinking. I blurted out asking if he had second thoughts about what we had said, or done. He shook his head no over and over saying it couldn't have been any better.

He repeated to me that he was deeply in love with me and that had been for a while now. It was definitely not a one-night-drunkenness-to-just-sack-me-kind-of-talk either. I had to think about what he had just said, and knew right then that he had meant every word of it. It just took him some liquid courage to get it out, after he calmed down realizing what he had said, and how he had acted when we arrived home. Then he went into an apology for his jealous streak and rage, saying he really didn't mean what he had said last night about me getting out. He just didn't know what else to say. He was hurting, definitely drunk, and he was jealous I had danced with all those guys. He knew he had made a big error in judgment by not sharing his feelings with me sooner. He was so mad at himself to think he was going to lose me, and just reacted with anger at me instead of telling me his true feelings.

I told him it would have been heavenly to have danced

with him the entire night, and I didn't know why he hadn't asked me. I had been so disappointed. I had to ask him on the last dance, which was the only ladies choice dance they had announced. And, that was exactly what it was, **my** choice. I chose him to be **my** dance partner, not anyone else there. Drew looked at me as if it finally clicked in his brain just how right I had been. He had been a drunk blinded fool that stewed about me dancing with other guys holding me in their arms when all he had to do was ask me. He hugged me telling me what happened last night at the reception, and what he had said afterwards, will never ever happen again. I accepted his apology. How could I not? I was in love with this man, and we had just opened our hearts to each other on how we truly felt.

We laid there in bed talking about everything under the sun, about each other between little kisses, and how we were feeling at the moment. It wasn't anything sexual right then, but it was really a very precious moment for me. We finally got up from the bed after deciding we needed to get some breakfast. Drew went to his house to shower, and put clean clothes on, while I showered, and dressed. I was walking up the his house just as he was coming out the back door so we could go to breakfast. Drew was staring at me smiling the entire time. He told me he couldn't take his eyes off of me walking towards him. I had to have blushed, as he opened the car door for me to get in. Just as I was about to get in the car he stopped me, giving me another deep kiss, and called me beautiful.

After breakfast, we rode down to the park along the shores of Lake Erie. We had taken the girls there a few times to play in the water at the beach during the summer. We couldn't stay there long enjoying the late summer breeze because Vivian's parents would be dropping the girls off in a few hours. So, we just sat on the swing under the pavilion talking about the girls until we had to leave. I could do it over and over again like that moment. Just sitting there with Drew at my side holding my hand and talking.

We decided to keep our relationship on a low key for awhile. Not like we had with the pregnancies, but we decided to gradually let the ball fall this time when telling people. We didn't want it to be a big secret as before, but we also didn't know how the family on both sides would feel about us dating each other.

Drew had told his mom that he had someone he had started to date when they had talked on the phone a few weeks ago. He said she seemed very pleased to hear that he had moved on with his life. He didn't say anything more about it. But when Carolyn and I were in the kitchen talking one afternoon when they came for a visit, Carolyn told me that Drew had been dating someone or that he wanted to date someone, she couldn't remember. I just looked at her when she asked if I knew that. I was sure I had the deer-in-the-headlights look on my face or not.

A week later she brought that same topic up again, and asked the same question if I knew who that person could be. I told her I wasn't exactly sure who it was. She took me by surprise by telling me she had wished it was me he was dating. I wondered why would she say that! I looked up at her to read her face. She stared at me with a puzzled looked across her face asking again if I knew who it could be. I quietly whispered to her it was me that he was dating.

Her face lit up, and her mouth opened as I heard her say, "it's you?". She put both her hands to her heart with this huge smile across her face. I could tell she was happy. When I nodded yes, she jumped off her chair to come give me a big hug. She said she had hoped for some time now that Drew would open his eyes, and see what a wonderful person I was, and how much I loved the girls. She asked if anyone else knew. I told her we hadn't told anyone yet. No a single soul. She was very happy for us. All that worrying I had done was for nothing!

When Drew and Mark walked in the house from playing a round of golf, I saw the twinkle in Carolyn's eyes as she asked Drew what was this person like that he was dating. He stopped frozen in his place as if he was six years old, and had been caught with his hand in the cookie jar. At first he tried to change the subject, but Carolyn was persistent by asking him again. He said she was a beautiful person inside and out, and thought she would be the kind of person that she would most likely approve of. He looked at me, and I had the best poker face of all time looking back at him. Carolyn wanted to know more, but Drew tried to avoid her questioning by talking about his golf game. Finally he asked his mom what difference did it make on who he was dating.

Carolyn had cocked her head saying that she had hoped he had opened his eyes to what was right in front of him. Mark piped up asking why all the questions to Drew. Carolyn said that Drew had told her he has been dating someone, and that he had a lot of feelings for this person. Mark looked at Drew with his eyes opened wide asking if that was true, about what his mother had just said. Drew acknowledged that it was. Then Mark started questioning him as Carolyn sat there grinning from ear to ear watching Drew squirm with his answers to his father. Finally, Drew told them enough with all the questions. He wasn't a teenager trying to date someone they might not approve of, and finally told them he was dating me.

Mark looked at me, and I nodded it was true. The smile that came across his face was heart warming. He patted Drew on the back telling him it was about time he saw in me what they had seen a long time ago. Carolyn confessed that she just found out herself, and had to pry it out me that I was the one he was dating. Drew came over putting his arm around me stating that he was glad they approved of his choice. Mark was very happy, and hugged us both saying he couldn't be any more happier for us as he was right then. We added that the girls haven't been told directly about us dating, but I have been with them at every function and outing, so we hoped they wouldn't think anything about us being together.

We weren't sure how Vivian's parents would take it though, but we didn't want to have them find out from anyone else. We planned to tell them when they brought the girls home later that day. They were the ones that might have something to say about it since Vivian was their daughter.

We lucked out when we told them our news. At first I thought they were going to get up and leave, but when they got up, they came over to us telling us how happy they were giving us a big hug each. They said they had talked about the chances of Drew marrying again, and that the both of them had hoped it would be with me. But, there didn't seem to be any indication that we were interested in each other. They felt they knew, and had already loved me, so it was making logical sense to them. Finally, Vivian's dad looked at Drew asking him what took him so long? They could think of no other person that they would have wanted to fill the shoes of their daughter, than me. They were very happy for us.

After they had left, both Drew and I knew a big load had been lifted off our shoulders with both sets of parents being happy for us. I couldn't explain how much better I was feeling about them knowing, and especially of their acceptance. We didn't have to hide our feelings toward each other in front of them any longer. Now to tell the siblings. I wasn't sure how Vivian's sisters would react, but I would soon find out. We were having the final cook out of the year next weekend with everyone, and planned to tell them then.

It was the first time I had dreaded the cook out since I started living there. I don't know if it was because of Vivian's sisters and their families were coming, or what everyone was going to think of me and Drew as a couple. Drew said he didn't care what they might think, say, or do because this was our time to shine. He never knew that I had overheard Vivian's sisters saying what they had on that day when he and Vivian announced they were pregnant again, with Avery in my belly. This dating news will probably blow their minds completely. Wish I felt better about them coming, and I wished I could be a fly on the wall when we tell everyone.

It wasn't until just before everyone was about to arrive that I thought differently about everything, and about everyone's opinion on us being a couple. Not too many people can say they had delivered two babies, and had never slept with a man ahead of time. And, from all the things Vivian had shared with me about her sisters, well….they had no room to talk about Drew and me being a couple. The many skeletons in their closets weren't anything to be proud of! The best thing is that I know so many of their family secrets from Vivian. Her sisters never come around to visit, but they'd show up for the cook outs and holidays all the time. Why not? It was a free meal for them! And, they didn't have to cook themselves.

After we were finished with our food that afternoon, I started to clean some of the dishes off the table. Drew came over putting his arm around my waist hugging me, and it turned dead silent behind us. We slowly turned around with everyone just staring at us with their mouths hanging open. It was Susan that spoke first asking if there was something they didn't know about that maybe we should share with them. Drew pulled me closer to him as he said he has been dating someone very special. I looked at Vivian's sisters, and could see them seething. They definitely weren't happy at what had just transpired. Susan jumped up to hug us saying she was so happy we were dating. She couldn't have asked for a better person for her brother than me. The shock had worn off, and others finally came up to congratulate us. Everyone, but Vivian's sisters.

Susan asked her mom if she had known already, and she had told her yes saying that they thought it was absolutely wonderful. Even Vivian's parents commented that they were just as happy for us as well. Shortly after everyone had found out, the sisters had to suddenly leave, and left in a hurry. It had turned out to be a great time after all, especially once the sisters had left.

The next day Carolyn came to my house early in the morning to invite me out to breakfast with the family. As I was dressing she asked if I had noticed how Vivian's sisters had acted when they found out Drew and I had been dating each other. I told her I had noticed, and I didn't think they were very happy about it. She told me they weren't happy one iota. She had overheard them in the house saying that they thought Drew was rushing into something he needed to think twice about when they retrieved their covered dish that they had brought. And, they wanted to know why the big rush wondering if I was pregnant again. Wow! They were bitter about it for sure. Carolyn apologized for telling me, and for overhearing their conversation. I told her I had overheard them talking about Vivian and Drew one time. They were just cranky jealous sisters. They weren't happy with their lives, and they didn't want anyone else to be happy either. Carolyn assured me their entire family was very happy for us, and Vivian's sisters could just kiss our ass.

I said that I had just hoped they're still nice to the girls when they are at Vivian's parents house on the weekends they stay over. Avery will tell us if they aren't. That girl is so wise when it comes to how people are treating them. She observes more than people think she does. She saw Drew sneaking a kiss from me one day, and asked if we were going steady. Wherever she heard that phrase before was beyond us. I had to chuckle, and we told her we were. Drew asked if it was okay with her that we were "going steady", and she said it made her very happy. Drew said he was glad she was happy. Ansley said she was happy too as she was getting in on the conversation we were having. It sure made it easier for me and Drew to not have to sneak around so the girls wouldn't see anything, or question us on anything. We were caught, and everything was out in the open now. Oh, how I loved that!! It made life easier for all of us.

I found a kindergarten class for Avery to attend a few days after the busy weekend we had was over. She was pretty excited about going to school. I made it a big deal of her going by taking her clothes shopping, letting her pick out her own backpack, and having lunch with her at her favorite cafe before attending a matinee showing an old favorite story of hers, 'Charlotte's Web'.

That night Drew said we needed to have dinner out with the girls to celebrate Avery starting school in less than two weeks. Sounded great to me. Drew picked out a very nice restaurant that was very posh. I knew I needed to have the girls dress in their pretty party dresses for that special place. When I walked out from my bedroom, Drew was at the door ready to come in. He looked at me saying maybe we should just stay right where we are with the two of us having a special celebration of our own. He winked at me, which I knew what he was referring to. Avery pulled Drew down to her level, and whispered we couldn't do that, it would ruin the surprise. Drew stood back up, and said Avery thinks we need to go out to eat. So, he said I looked beautiful as he was holding out his hand for me to take as we walked out the house. As soon as we had secured the girls in their car seats we were on our way.

As we were escorted to our seats in the restaurant, I gazed around the room. Wow! This place was extremely nice, and I had a feeling it was also extremely expensive. I thought the place was a bit overboard to go to just to celebrate Avery going to school though. Drew insisted I order whatever I wanted. I had never eaten at a place like this before, and noticed immediately that there weren't any dollar amounts on the menu. I whispered over to Drew that my menu didn't come with the prices listed. He told me that people who had to ask for the prices didn't belong in a place as nice as this to begin with, and not to worry about the prices. Another wow! I let him order the girls meal while I waited for Drew to give his order before I told the waiter I would have the same as he was having. Steak and lobster tail sounded good to me, too.

I couldn't believe how delicious everything tasted. The steak was so tender I didn't have to cut it with the knife. Both the steak and lobster just melted in my mouth. I knew there wasn't any room for dessert for me, so Drew asked the waiter for the tiramisu to be boxed for us to take home. Drew also ordered a bottle of champagne which the waiter brought to the table immediately. The waiter poured it into two fluted glasses before stepping away. I thought Drew was getting the girls ready to leave without drinking the champagne when he took Ansley out of the booster seat she was in. They came around to where they could face me directly. Ansley handed me a red rose telling me she loved me, and gave me a kiss followed by Avery. I took the roses, and they went to their dad getting down on one knee like Drew was.

The next thing I knew all three of them were asking me to marry them at the same time. I sat back in my chair as I wasn't expecting that to happen, but it sure explained going to dinner at this place now. I knew I had tears welling up in my eyes by then, and I nodded yes, yes I would marry them, all three of them. I kissed Drew when he placed the ring on my finger. Drew must have practiced this over and over with the girls for them to do it so smoothly.

Everyone around us clapped and congratulated us. They thought that was the most precious proposal they had ever seen. Then one lady asked if we were the people she had read about in the newspaper last year. Drew said it could be. The lady took my hand telling me that she thought I was the most bravest person she had ever heard of, and now she had met me. She had said this loud enough for others to hear, and they all clapped.

When Drew sat back in his chair, he had wanted to make a quiet toast to me, for accepting their proposal of marriage. He made a beautiful toast, and we drank our glass of champagne while the girls drank their ginger ale. One other person in the same room watching us, stood up tapping his wine glass with his spoon announcing that he wanted to make a toast to us as well, if we didn't mind. Drew nodded his head that it was fine. The man had everyone's attention as he started out by wishing us the best life has to offer, and hoped we have a wonder life together. We had been through a horrific situation resulting in me being a hero saving the little girls lives, as well as my own life. Suddenly, everyone held up their glasses saying "here here" to us before drinking their own drink. We thanked him, and everyone else for their kindness. When we got up to leave, many of the people came over giving us a hug, and more blessed wishes for a long happy life together. It was the most beautiful night of my life.

The girls were changed out of their party dresses, and in bed in a matter of minutes once we arrived home. Drew pulled me over to him for a kiss as we both kissed the girls goodnight. That night was the first time I stayed over in Drew's house while the girls were there. It just felt so natural for me to be there, and I sure was never going to question the reason it had all happened. I just knew it was right.

# MORE GOOD NEWS

—⊰·•————————◆————————•·⊱—

Drew and I talked for a few hours before we fell asleep that night after making love for the second time. Every time I held my hand up to the moonlight peaking in through the window, I gazed at my ring, as I quietly gushed over it. It was very exquisite. I already knew Drew had wonderful taste in jewelry from the necklaces he had picked out a while back for me, but my engagement ring was over the top as far as I was concerned. It was the most beautiful ring I had ever seen. And, the most important part was that Drew had asked me to be his wife. Well, Drew and the girls did actually. I couldn't have been any happier than what I am feeling now. I felt I had been truly blessed. I am engaged to the man I love, and to his two beautiful daughters who mean so much to me.

Drew, and I made breakfast the following morning

consisting of pancakes and fruit. We weren't finished eating when Carolyn and Mark showed up to join us. They had been in town the past few days house hunting. They sold their house in their town, and needed to find one here. They had talked about moving here several months ago once they both were retired, so they could be closer to Drew and the girls, and only about forty-five minutes away from Susan. We were all glad they had decided to move closer. They had found a house that they thought checked off all their wants and needs, but they wanted us to look at it before they signed on the dotted line.

Drew had to laugh when we pulled in the driveway of the house his parents wanted us to look at with them. It was a mere three houses from us. Drew wondered out loud if they thought they were going to be too close to us. Mark said, "nonsense", with a wink to me. The house was much smaller than their other house, which was great for them. They needed to downsize at their age, and this was a great size for them. It was a nice spacious house with plenty of land to keep them busy, and they would be close to us.

Once back at our house, funny how I was already referring to it as our house, and not Drew's house, Mark wanted to know if we had decided when to tie the knot. They didn't want their move into another house to be at the same time we had wanted to get married. The wedding was more important to them. I knew they were just trying to be considerate, and I appreciated that. I asked when they thought they'd be moving. Carolyn said they had to be out of their house in less than a month, so they're hoping the house that they want, will be available for them to move right into. So they wouldn't have to waste time moving everything into storage to move everything back out of storage in a few weeks. Made sense, and I knew there was no way we would be getting married that soon.

I told them they didn't have to worry about the dates coinciding because we hadn't talked about a date ourselves. Mark was the first to tell Drew that he better not drag his feet in making an honest woman out of me, and winked at me. Drew asked him where did he come up with all these corny sayings. I had to laugh, shaking my head.

Funny how Mark had said that because I had thought Drew and I needed to talk about it ourselves. I didn't want a long engagement, but I didn't want one rushed either. I would need to have a little time to plan everything.

I offered to help Carolyn pack their house whenever they got the news on the house three houses down the road from us, that they had put an offer on. Mark said the house was vacant, and the owners were motivated to get it sold, so it might be soon that they can move in. As it turned out, they got the house, and the previous owners said they could transfer the ownership over to them at any time. Great news there! Mark and Carolyn could move right in sooner than what they had thought. We decided that I would ride back with Mark and Carolyn on Thursday when they leave, and help them start packing right away. Drew could come on the weekend, while the girls were at Vivian's parent's house for the weekend, to help with the rest of the packing, and I would go back with Drew when we were done. It worked out perfect for everyone.

The following weekend, Drew went back to their house to help them load everything into the moving truck. The girls and I stayed home that weekend, but I prepared a large meal for everyone, because I knew they would be hungry when they were done unloading everything in their new home.

Once Mark and Carolyn were finally settled into their home, and had the other one cleared out completely, we could then make plans concerning our wedding. Drew asked me if we could get it planned in time for an autumn wedding. I thought it was do-able, so we picked the weekend we wanted, and I started working towards our plans. Carolyn was a gem helping me because she offered some great ideas. Within a week I had contacted everyone necessary, and Drew and I chose, and ordered the invitations. We had five weeks to pull it off, and I knew in my heart we would have the most beautiful wedding ever imaginable. Everything was going to happen right there in the backyard. Simple, and yet elegant! I had thought about asking Carolyn to go gown shopping with me, but changed my mind thinking I wanted to do this on my own.

I didn't have a mother to share this special time of my life with when I thought about it. My mother hadn't been a part of my life since I was twelve, and I didn't want her to think she could come back into my life now if she knew I was getting married. I was happy with my life the way it was, and about to marry the man I was deeply in love with. During the time, after she sent me away, she never made any contact with me to see if I needed anything, or inquire on how I was doing. Not even to the place I was living at. I didn't need her now. I wasn't the same person from long ago. I had grown into a loving, kind, and generous person. I don't think she would believe that about me anyhow, even if she had been a part of my life. But, she had made the choice to get rid of me, and I am a better person for it. I have no regrets with myself, or my life. I had moved on.

Drew and I had decided to set the chairs in the yard for the people to sit in during the wedding part, leaving the patio open for the reception. Decorations were part of the package deal with the cater we had hired, which was a huge help. The disc jockey claimed his area that he would need when he came to look the place over. Drew and I had our license already, just waiting for our day to arrive. Both the girls dresses had arrived, and fit them perfectly. I had asked Susan to be my maid of honor, and her dress would arrive in a few days. Drew's dad was standing in for Drew as the best man. Drew's dad was so honored that he had asked him to be his best man, but when we thought about it, Mark wasn't just his dad. He **was** his best friend. We just needed for the day to get there!

As the days rolled off the calendar bringing us closer to our wedding, we kept our eyes on the weather. So far every day that week was going to be warm, and sunny for our wedding. Everyone was up early that morning to get everything ready. Susan came a few days before, and was staying at my little house, so she could help out. The cater had everything ready, disc jockey was ready, and the people that did the decorations were set. The backyard had been turned into the most beautiful scene for our wedding. I couldn't have been any happier.

People arriving had remarked how beautiful everything was. Susan had the girls dressed in their gowns, and handed them their baskets filled with rose petals to drop as they walked down the isle to the front. They were going to sit with Carolyn when they were done. Susan turned to me saying she was so happy for the both of us, and that her brother did good. She hugged me while telling me I was going to knock the socks off Drew when he sees me in my gown. We talked a few minutes of girl talk. I confessed I was nervous, and shaking like a leaf ready to fall off a tree. Drew and Vivian had been the best thing that ever came into my life, and I planned on making Drew the happiest man on earth. Susan looked at me saying she thought I had already done that before grabbing my bouquet of flowers to hand to me. She grabbed her bouquet stating that we needed a minute to get composed because it was time. Susan did another three hundred sixty degree walk around me stating that I looked absolutely beautiful, and we were now ready to go!

I watched from the window as the girls walked down the isle dropping the rose petals along the way. The photographer took several pictures of them before they sat down with their grandmother. Susan looked radiant when she walked to the front to take her place next to me. I didn't know if my knees would hold me up much longer. Then the door was opened for me to walk out while the bridal march played, and everyone stood up.

I managed to get down the isle, but only because of Drew. When I saw him I knew everything felt as if it was meant to be for us. Susan had been right about Drew, though. The look Drew had for me when he saw me was something I will never forget. It melted my heart. Mark gave Drew a little nudge with his elbow, whispering to Drew that I was absolutely the most stunning bride he had ever seen. As soon as I reached Drew he took my hand whispering in my ear on how gorgeous I was with a quick, "I love you" to follow. I smiled when I whispered that I was so in love with him, and loved him more than what I had ever dreamed I could love someone. He planted a small kiss on my cheek before we turned toward the minister to have him perform the ceremony. Every chance Drew could, he kissed my fingertips until we had been pronounced husband and wife. He pulled me quickly into his arms planting his lips on to mine as we sealed our vows.

We were officially married now, and everyone cheered for us. Everyone except Vivian's sisters. Why did they even bother to come I wondered, if they weren't happy for us. Well, I wasn't going to let them put a damper on my wedding. I was kind to them when they came up to congratulate us, but basically ignored them the rest of the time. Vivian's parents were happy for us, and I could tell they meant it. I could also tell that they had seen how their daughters had reacted during the ceremony as well. They didn't look too pleased with them.

Just before we started to eat our dinner, Drew's dad gave a fabulous toast to us. That was followed by Vivian's dad. It was also nice. I looked at Vivian's sisters, and they weren't happy. The oldest one stood up asking how could he give a toast like he had to us. It wasn't right to give a toast to his former son-in-law, and his new wife. She felt it was betraying their sister by doing so.

Their mother was quick to answer her daughter by saying that Vivian would have approved of Drew and I being married one hundred per cent. She added that Vivian would also be so disappointed in both of them, and they needed to accept the fact that Drew had every right to more happiness, to be in love again, and that I was the happiness and love he deserved. The anger and disgust shown by the girls was obvious, as they abruptly got up leaving with their family in tow. I stood there in shock not knowing what to say. It was silent outside among the other guest. Even the birds had quit chirping. I wasn't sure what to do until Vivian's father apologized, and said to continue on with the reception.

After the dinner, and with the cake cut and served, we got down to enjoying the rest of the night dancing, and having a great time. I told Drew he had better save some dances for me this time. He said he would save every one of them for me if he could. We knew that was going to be impossible, but he promised he'd dance as much as he could with me. And he did. We danced the night away. Even after everyone and the vendors had left, we danced one last dance together under the harvest moon. It was the most romantic dance I had the entire evening.

I could have stayed outside enjoying it all night, but leaving early in the morning for Disney World with the girls for our honeymoon, we needed our sleep. It was going to be a long day. We had choose to celebrate our honeymoon as a family, and what better place to go to was the happiest place on earth, Disney World! The girls were thrilled with that plan. So, we made the most of our honeymoon night. We were both exhausted in the morning, but decided we'd take turns sleeping on the plane.

Our honeymoon with the girls couldn't have been any better than what it was. We had a great time! It was so different in one aspect that we were going there as a family, and yet we have done so many other things together I hadn't thought of it as being any different. But now, we're a bona fide family. Our honeymoon week in Florida was over before we knew it, and we were on a plane to return to our home. Our home sounded so nice.

While we were gone for the week, Mark had asked us if we minded if he went into the attic to search for those papers, and that ledger he had remembered seeing up there. We didn't mind at all. In fact, we were curious if there was some vital information on the house and tunnel, and what the ledger could reveal on anything, if he could find them. It had been over fifteen years since he had seen them, so it might be a waste of time now. It gave Drew and me something to talk about on the flight home. Both girls had fallen asleep shortly on our laps after taking off, giving us time to talk without tending to them.

Drew was as excited as I was to see if the house held some good historical information. It wasn't custom to have a tunnel underground just to have one. There had to be a reason for it being meticulously built, and I was determined that I would find the answers as to why. Drew thought maybe we'd find some answers through the housing department, or even the road planning commission. If we could find a name attached to the property, that would help us with our search.

Well, we didn't have to look for any information right away. Drew sent me a dozen red roses for our one month wedding anniversary. The delivery guy handed me the roses asking how I liked living there. I said we loved the place, and smiled as I thanked him for the delivery. He told me his great great grandparents built both houses. Both houses? I needed to talk to him a little bit more since he knew there were two houses on the property. I invited him in right away to chat for a few minutes. He said his grandparents had sold the house, and property when he was a teenager. They didn't want to keep it in the family any longer, and he didn't have any means of purchasing it at his young age. He had to leave right away to finish his deliveries, so I asked him and his wife to come to dinner the following night so Drew would be able to be there to hear him talk about the house. He was kind enough to give me his name, and phone number before leaving, saying he would just love to see what had been done to the house since he had stayed there as a kid. As he was heading out the door he asked me if I had found the secrets the house held yet, and winked. I said I had found one asking if there were more. He just smiled as he walked away. I couldn't wait to tell Drew that night about him.

In the meantime I got on the computer using his last name to see if I could trace backwards any information, but was unsuccessful. Mark had come by later that day, and I told him what the floral delivery guy had told me. Mark rubbed his hands together saying we needed to find the papers right then, and that ledger, too. Ansley was down for her afternoon nap, so Mark and I went to the attic to search more. No luck, until we were headed back down the stairs that I saw something between the beams that had a layer of dust covering it making it barely visible. I found what we had been searching for, finally. Mark and I about stumbled going down the stairs as fast as possible, so we could open the envelopes as soon as possible.

The paper in the ledger was so fragile we had to turn each, and every page carefully. There were names, and dates on several pages. Some had large X's which made both Mark and I wonder if the people couldn't write their names, or maybe they didn't want to write their names. This book was dated back to 1855, and it looked as if it was part of the Underground Railroad after all. There were other things written towards the back of the ledger as well.

Apparently, the first owner of the house were ardent abolitionists who had assisted enslaved people on their paths to freedom. There were several homes in the area that had places for the slaves to hide in during the day to be safe, until after dark when they made their journey towards freedom. Owners provided them with meals, and a place to sleep while they waited for night fall, so they could continue on their journey. That might explain why there was a room-like portion at the end of the tunnel on my end. Maybe more people could hide in it without it being crowded. It was also written that many of the enslaved people had written their names on the walls. I never noticed any names when I had been in the tunnel, but then again, I hadn't been looking for any. So much information this beautiful old ledger held.

We opened the other paper that was rolled up with a rotting leather band tied around it. Carefully we unrolled it on the counter, and it contained blueprints of the little house, big house and the entire property. That was when we saw the tunnel from house to house, plain as day. It looked as if our tunnel had been built during the time the larger home was being constructed. Who ever drew the tunnel on the paper had wrote a date across it. It was amazing to think we had found some valuable information. And to think how historical our house actually was.

We couldn't wait for Drew to get home to share everything with him. Carolyn came down to the house after Mark had called her to tell her about the stuff we had found. She was just as excited as we were. To think that the owners had provided a safe place for the enslaved people, but it had also been a safe place for me and the girls, too. I thought how great it would be to have photographs to add, but we didn't find any.

I noticed the time, and knew Drew would be home soon. I was running late in starting our dinner meal. Carolyn came to my rescue stating she had made a large amount of stuffed bell peppers that day. She planned on filling her freezer for the winter months with the fresh peppers. She had more than enough in the oven, so she invited us down there for dinner. I knew Drew wouldn't mind that either. He absolutely loved his mother's stuffed peppers.

After dinner, the girls went out back to play on the jungle gym that had been left at their house. They had a great time on it while the four of us talked about what Mark and I had found earlier, and what the delivery guy had told me. Told Drew that the delivery guy and his wife were going to join us for dinner the next night. I invited Carolyn and Mark to dinner also. We were pretty pumped about the information we had found earlier, and the information we could learn about tomorrow.

Drew made it home a little bit earlier than normal to help with dinner. Carolyn had been marinating the steaks, and chicken all day for Drew to grill later. Edward showed up with his wife right on time bringing a bottle of wine with them to share. I quickly introduced everyone. Edward's wife's name was Ginny, and she was also very nice. While the guys went onto the patio for Drew to start the grilling, we talked in the living room about things in general.

After dinner I put the girls in bed for the night so we could dive into the tunnel business that we were anxious to find more information about. Edward went to his car, and brought in a small box of items he had of the house from his great great grandparents things stored in his basement. He almost threw everything away until Ginny had suggested that the new owners of this house might like to have them. They hadn't met us at that time, and had considered just dropping everything off on the porch by the front door at one time. I pulled a few things out to examine closely, and then passed them on to the others. There were pictures, journals, and written official documents that included several names. It was the best treasure to hold all these wonderful pieces of history on the house and the entire community. I asked if I could keep a few things to read, and copy. Edward said everything was mine to keep. I just stared at him with disbelief written across my face. How generous of him to give everything to us! I couldn't thank him enough for it!

He said he knew we had found the tunnel from what he had read in the paper about our incident earlier. He said he was glad the girls had been kept safe in the tunnel. He also informed us many of the enslaved people were hidden in the attic as well, in an area that wasn't expected. He showed us on the blueprint that I had spread open on the coffee table where it was located. He said he remembered his father talking about playing in it on rainy days when he was a very little boy. There was so much information to absorb that we had lost track of time until the grandfather clock chimed one in the morning. We could have gone on longer, but their babysitter had to get home by two at the latest.

We made another dinner date for the following Saturday afternoon, and they were to bring their little girls with them this time. Their girls were pretty close to Avery and Ansley's age, and I knew they would have a great time playing together.

After Carolyn and Mark left, I hurried up cleaning the remainder of the kitchen dishes with Drew's help, before we went to bed ourselves. Did we get much sleep? Nope!! We were so pumped up about all the information in the box we couldn't stop talking about everything. Drew nudged me saying all this was all my fault, as he smiled, and winked at me. We talked about the what "if's" that this all meant, and if it was true, where do we go from here. I thought it was extremely important that people recognize this place for what it had been back then. Our house had played an important part of the history of the Underground Railroad.

We became great friends with Edward and Ginny, all due to this house. Carolyn and Mark were pretty excited when we found several photographs of the local area growing. There were several pictures looking towards Carolyn and Mark's house that we could see how it had been built. The lumber was made right in the backyard with a mill cutting the logs into the lumber. Logs that had been dragged to the site by horses from the wooded area close to the property. We were a little disappointed that their house wasn't part of the Underground

Railroad, though.

We went to the monthly town council meeting after we had all our facts lined up, to have our house registered as a historical home. We presented everything we had by using a power presentation of all the documents, photographs, and written testimony by what the people had stated in the journals. We had a month to wait for their decision on what they would or wouldn't agree to, and that drove us crazy.

The day we went back to the city council meeting I had been to the doctor's office earlier for what I had suspected. I was pregnant. I was going to have a baby, and couldn't be happier. I wanted to tell everyone right away, but not sure how Drew felt about having another baby. I wasn't sure when I would tell him the news either. This baby would be our baby which had made me extra happy. I just needed to tell him when the time was right.

That night at the meeting we found out our house had been approved to be classified as a historical house, and the Underground Railroad was indeed an authentic part of the history to the community as well. Of course we were all ecstatically happy with that news. We decided to stop by the cafe to celebrate. Drew had been blabbering on and on how important that day had been for all of us. I casually announced that I was pregnant between all the chatter happening. It took a minute for Drew to comprehend what I had just blurted out. He stopped talking about the house, and slowly turned to me asking if he had heard me right. I nodded, and he cheered loud enough to have everyone's attention in the cafe. I was relieved that he was happy. Carolyn and Mark were just as happy for us, too. We had two things to celebrate that night, and even though I hadn't planned for any of these things to happen like they had, I was glad they did. Drew looked at me again to make sure he heard what I had said correctly before he kissed me, again and again. He said he had hoped we'd have a baby together, and now we are.

# ℰPILOGUE

<hr>

As the old saying goes, "life goes on", and our lives went on as well. We were no longer a family of four, we are now a family of six. Angela and Andrew Jr. were added to the family making the family complete within a few years after Drew and I had married.

Drew's business prospered immensely over the years that he had to add other attorneys, and expand the office size. I couldn't have been more proud of him. Did the Jones brothers situation help with that? We aren't sure, but it was known what had happened at our house on that dreadful day by everyone who came into the office for help on their own situation.

I may have had a rough beginning in my life, but I wouldn't change what I have now for anyone, or anything in the world. My life has been great being married to

Drew. His love was more than what I had ever expected to find. We raised a wonderful family that have remained close to us, and to each other. The two girls that Drew had with Vivian, my best friend, and the two we had together ourselves.

Over the years Vivian's parents were the only ones attending our Saturday cookouts on a regular basis along with Drew's entire side of the family. Vivian's sisters quit coming to them after Drew and I had married. They had told everyone that Drew was no longer related to them, just the little girls, so they did not attend anymore of our cookouts. Drew was fine with that, which really surprised me. I had talked with Vivian's parents to see if there was a way I could help keep the family together. They both felt their daughters were making a big mistake feeling the way they did, but their daughters were entitled to their opinions, and feelings. However, that wasn't how they themselves had felt towards us at all. They were very grateful at how happy I had made their daughter when she was alive by helping her become the mom she had desperately wanted to be. It had been her greatest accomplishment by becoming a mother, and they had felt blessed having Vivian's two beautiful girls as a reminder of their daughter whenever they saw them.

As far as we were concerned, Vivian's parents were still part of the family, and that they would be invited to everything that involved their granddaughters.

As for the tunnel, with all the information I had received from Edward, and what was in our attic, I wrote a book about everything. I felt it was something that needed to be in print for people to read, and recognize how this area was such an important part of the Underground Railroad. There were so many photographs in the box that Edward had given me that maybe, just maybe, someone would recognize an ancestor, and they would have some history about their family to pass on, or a story about someone they had recognized. I could only hope for that.

Drew and I had opened the basement in our house to let people go through the tunnel all the way to the little house for the ultimate experience of what it had been like for people to gain their freedom from slavery in our area. We had a door from the basement to the outside installed making the access easier. The little house I had lived in was converted into a mini museum with the photographs enlarged to hang on the walls for everyone to see. I also sold many copies of my book on the historical importance of the place. I wanted the house to shine with the way it had played a part in the history of that era.

One guest that came through the tunnel had looked familiar to me, but I didn't know where or why until he signed the guest book. Once he had entered the tunnel I had to see what name he had written. I had to look twice thinking I had read it wrong the first time. I then knew why he looked familiar to me. He was my father! He obviously didn't know it was me, and I wasn't sure if I should say anything to him before he left. He hadn't seen me for over thirty years now, and I was probably out of his mind completely. But, I now had his address. He was still living in Virginia a few towns away from where he walked out of my life when I was six years old. Maybe I will write to him letting him know who I am. And then again, maybe I shouldn't dredge up the hurtful memories I have had to live with. I don't think I could go through another heartbreak like I did when I was six. As far as I knew he had never tried to find me, and I had made no effort on my part to find him. I thought it was best to let it be as it was.

I sent out Christmas cards each year to all the people who had toured our home by going through the tunnel that had left their addresses in the guest book. I purposely had sent one to my father's house every single year, even though he hadn't been back since that first time. I never heard back from him, until several years down the road when I received a letter.

The letter was from my dad's wife, Agnes. She was wondering the reason for me to send a Christmas card to her husband the past few years, and she thought maybe she knew the reason without having to say anything more. She had asked for me to call her sometime to discuss it. I talked it over with Drew that night, and he thought he should check into it himself before I went any further with the idea of calling that lady back. So many people are doing scams on other people that Drew didn't want me to fall victim to one. Drew had done the research I needed, and he informed me that she was legit, and yes, he was my father.

I called her one afternoon when I was alone in the house, and introduced myself to her. She was very happy

I had called. Her husband wasn't there at the moment, but she asked if there was a possibility that I could be his daughter from his first marriage. I acknowledged that I was pretty certain that I was. I heard her take a deep breath as she told me my father had done everything he could to find me, but he could never get any information. He was heartbroken that he had left me behind when he walked out on us. He said I hadn't deserve that. I hadn't done anything wrong. But my mother had, and it hurt him deeply when she kicked him out of the house.

Agnes assured me that he was going to be very excited that we had found each other after all these years of semi-searching. She continued to explain that he had searched for years to locate me, but had never been successful. The courts wouldn't help him saying the records had been sealed, and his ex-wife had threatened to call the police on him if he ever showed up at her house again asking her questions. My father had wrote me a letter at great length explaining everything, and she told me that he never quit loving me. He still had the little bracelet that I had made for him out of string when I was five years old at summer camp. We agreed to meet sometime, but until then, she would be happy to mail me the letter and bracelet now. I couldn't wait to receive them, and we set a date for all of us to meet.

After setting a date for them to come for a visit, I was feeling like a whole lot of weight had been lifted off my shoulders. Drew was happy for me, and when the time came for my dad and Agnes to visit us, I was on pins and needles. I had talked briefly a few times with my dad, but it isn't the same as it will be meeting him face to face once again after all the years we had missed out on being together.

The day they were to arrive, I got a phone call that broke my heart once again. It was Agnes. My dad had a heart attack while driving to our house, and was in the hospital about an hour away. I got the name and address of the hospital, and told Drew what had happened. It didn't take us more than a minute to get things settled at the house before we got in the car to drive to the hospital. I was so glad Drew was driving, and going to be with me.

As soon as we arrived there we were escorted directly to my dad's room. Agnes met us at the door saying he had been calling out my name. The doctors were not optimistic on his chances to recover. My dad looked so old in that bed hooked up to several machines. I asked if I could talk to him, and Agnes had said "absolutely".

I walked over to the bed taking his hand into mine as I kissed his cheek. I quietly told him who I was. He immediately squeezed my hand whispering he was so happy to see me. He told me I was so beautiful. As I was about to introduce him to Drew he squeezed my hand, and told me he loved me, as he closed his eyes. He was gone. Agnes said he waited for me to come before he would let go. He said he had to see me, and to tell me he had always loved me, and that he was sorry he could not find me. Drew was right behind me, and I turned to cry into his chest. I couldn't believe how we had finally found each other, and now he was taken away from me once again.

I was so sad, but I was also very grateful for finally knowing that I had been loved, and was never forgotten about.

# THE END

# About The Author

## Joann Buie

Joann was born and raised in Ashtabula, Ohio, and liked writing short stories and numerous poems for others to read. Two hours after graduating from high school, she moved to Michigan to be with her husband, Bo, who was serving in the Air Force.

Moving to Arizona in 1979 as a young mother of three, Joann went to work in the school district in the Special Education department while completing her Bachelor's Degree. She earned her Master's Degree from Northern Arizona University while teaching elementary education.

After over twenty years working in the educational field and living over forty years in Arizona, she retired and now resides in Florida with her husband and two little dogs, Charlie Brown and Lucy.

Joann has been married for over fifty years, has three grown children and is a grandmother to seven.

Other Books in the

*Small Town Romance Series*

by

Joann Buie

# Abby's Quest

Abby struggled with her life right from the beginning by living in one foster home after another, until she graduated from high school. Everyone had referred to her as the basket baby that had been abandoned at a fire station after her birth, which was difficult for her to overcome.

Knowing she wanted to escape from there, and her past, to make a fresh start with her life in another town or state, she accepted a house sitting job in Jasper, Tennessee, not knowing what to expect or what would be waiting for her around the corner.

This heart warming romance story will leave you wanting to find out more about Abby's life, and how it had been changed along the way.

# Sandy Dunes Resort

Lexi had lost her dream job and her fiancee, Phillip, in New York City on the same day. Now, she was worried about her safety because of his indiscretions and of the illegal banking information she had stumbled upon that Phillip had been doing to his clients. The only thing she could do now was get out of New York City fast and stay under the radar of Phillip's rage. Lexi would now return to her family's home in Michigan, where she thought she would be safe from Phillip, only to have him track her there. Little did she know that her first love was working at the resort where she had lived with her Aunt Sandy.

On Lexi's return home, her life becomes an up-and-down battle. She battles with her old New York life that continues to haunt her, and the new life she is seeking keeps her in constant turmoil. As she tries to plan her future, she uncovers things from the past that happened during her college years that become so devastating to her that she thinks it may be in her best interest to just move away from all her family and friends.

Will Lexi find a future and the love she desires so desperately?

# Small Town Happiness

Sadie Stanton worked five years teaching fourth grade students, and loving it every minute. It was a career she had chosen ever since she was in the fourth grade, all because of the teacher she had that made learning enjoyable and achievable. Sadie wanted to be like her by making learning fun, and interesting for her students.

After teaching for five years Sadie was about to quit her teaching career. She had worked hard, and the kids responded with most of them reaching or exceeding the State Standards each year. The problem was that a lot of her co-workers resented her. They felt she was making them look bad, and that put a target on Sadie's back. It made the workplace very uncomfortable and a hostile place for Sadie, to say the least.

Not certain what it would be like if she was to leave what she thought was her dream job, and now not knowing if she would ever want to teach again, but she knew she couldn't stay there any longer.

Sadie knew she was ready to begin a new chapter in her life. She decided she would search for a new job, in a new town, and a new start.

Would Sadie find what she wanted all her life or maybe that life some how would find her.